NOTES FROM A
DARK STREET

With all rigour I distinguish . . .
the instantly actual from the constantly
possible.

SPENGLER

NOTES FROM A
DARK STREET

Edward Adler

ALFRED·A·KNOPF   *NEW YORK*

1962

I DEDICATE THIS WORK TO MY WIFE,

Elaine,

who has sustained the weight of its aspirations

with sweet, good humor, and gentleness,

and a strength exceeding mine.

L. C. catalog card number: 61–14572

THIS IS A BORZOI BOOK,
PUBLISHED BY ALFRED A. KNOPF, INC.

FIRST EDITION

PART ONE

PART ONE

AUGUST

T HAT AFTERNOON A POWERFUL SUMMER STORM had struck the city. By midnight our streets were wholly stilled, crushed under a molten heat flowing earthward from the heavens. The sky, the stars, the long fine scarfs of cloud had acquired a low luminescence, like that of smoking dross, and a curious shine was put on the night.

Our drains were glutted behind the abnormal tide. Avenue C, on which I'd been walking home, served as a lock to the flotillas of sewage racing toward corner swells. The stores were dark. Here and there a yellow nightlight burned indoors, and an incandescence, greenish and pale, in the tones of a young greenpea pod, issued from the corner lamps. Window legends moved limply in this greenish mist, as if, melted to a syrup, they would this minute flow down the burning sheets of glass. I remember the progression of potted flowers in the variety store, their colors corrupted by the dark and mist. In the window of the Bramovitch shop, two plucked fowl hung head down, their cold pores so large they seemed to exist in some numerical arrangement. Under the fowl, two kittens slept, were starving, since the butcher had suffered a stroke, and I remember their filament whiskers sporting sawdust chips. Little Jenny, our janitor's daughter, had fallen in love with these kittens and every day, on her way home from school, she would stop at the butcher's window to witness their slow decrement. Between Ninth Street and Fifth, the meager file of peddler carts, broken by an occasional automobile, seemed pathetic and doltish. One cart was put together entirely of abandoned doors. Most of the carts were oppressed by thick tarpaulins tied down to the wobbly wheels, and these covers rose into high, shapeless dunes. You might have thought that the peddlers themselves were spending the night under canvas: Aza Luft, Propish, John Helm, August Turino, each huddled in his own cart dead asleep until dawn, when the market truckmen would arrive. Several carts were lit from beneath by suspended lamps, the large, masked kind I had always associated with Tartock, a neighbor. During the cold months, a majority of peddlers would spend their nights in a Suffolk Street steambath.

I had stopped at John Helm's cart. He was our neighborhood bladegrinder, a tall, brooding man with an uncommon skill, who was filled with the idea that the next generation would see the demise of his shining craft. Helm's cart was the best of all, of fine, white ash, daily scrubbed, with a superdeck of doweled, finished planks to house the grinding stones, and a silver motor deep within the cart's chassis. Life to Helm was not a temple of abstract hopes, but a chaos of arbitrary cruelties, in which each day struck him with increasing force. He had longed with all his heart to give over his skills with

the blade and shear to his young and only son, but the
boy was a moaning spastic; those little hands in tonic
spasm were disinherited entirely from Helm's legacy.
Often I'd seen and heard the boy cry and moan, his impotence upon him, for he was doomed to watch, only to
watch, the magical wheel of stars flying off his father's
flying stones. Helm brooded and cursed the world,
cursed the boy and his wife, cursed life and himself, until he seemed like a child lisping in innocence at the lip
of a grave. He would stalk the neighborhood sound-
lessly, deep into the night, hand-in-hand with anyone
who would accompany him, and sometimes he could be
seen walking over the bridge into Williamsburg, side-by-
side with Gilda Quastafesti, with her father close behind
them.

As I stood at his cart, remembering his promise to de-
stroy it when he became too old to work, a contorted figure moved slowly round the corner of Sixth Street; it
paused under the greenish spray of the corner lamp. As
it moved from shadow to light, I saw that it carried an
umbrella, which it utilized as a cane. The figure was
hooked and humped so badly that it formed almost the
whole of an inverted U. It ignored Helm's cart, at which
one usually stopped in admiration. It showed no interest in me, nor in any of the corner stores. In a minute
several more figures materialized out of Sixth Street,
and settled with their predecessor under the greenish
spray. There, in that hell of heat, a miracle of black frost
touched my heart. For this was still another nightly as-
semblage of homeless hags, a phenomenon prevailing
on our streets since the war's end. They were present,
everywhere present, on the rind of our neighborhood,
like unhealing sores. In time, I was to learn of my janitor's relation to these women. Perhaps he had imagined

that their sorority would soon receive Zena Cudcik, his wife's aged mother. They were makeshift, amorphous, possessing no logic of genesis, nor one of disintegration, and if they possessed an explicit identity, it consisted of that racking depletion of the body by malnutrition, and a certain deadly cast—an outward pallor of an inner malaise. Each one of them seemed to be waiting for our city to die.

Each spongy flat face was pulled like a sock over a boneless head, her pores were filled with our city's filth, her hair was stale with the loveless dust of her own neglect, her legs were so spavined from her walking, her gathering, they seemed freshly burst within. There was a bluishness to her skin, as if we lived only in a solitary climate of winter. Yet she moved about the streets mutely, almost shyly, and, despite her offensiveness, she moved with a certain swift femininity, playing at sensuality, swinging her hips with ridiculous excess, luxuriating her fingers through her hair, passing hands suggestively over a crabbed bosom, a fleshless flank. I've often seen a hag in her night's retirement, in a doorway, or sitting on a subway step, or in a neighborhood park, solemnly flattering and caressing her legs, in a fiction of pulling on her imaginary silk stockings. Quastafesti, the dollmaker, out of shreds of waste material had once created a stuffed likeness of this hag, detestable in its realism, for he was sure she was here only to mock us, yet was human enough to mock herself.

On Sixth Street this night, they rose out of their own fluids to gather on the corner, from doorways of their own considered selection, from condemned tenements and deserted lofts, from all the dips and twists our neighborhood offers. They were able, when night came, to utilize our terrain so effectively that they became organic parts of their covering lairs, and they were always passed by, free from the traditional harangue of chase and arrest. They were together now, on the corner, rooted, mute. Suddenly the avenue sprang alive. Here at midnight every store, every cart, produced its owner. On my walk through I hadn't noticed a soul. Or so it had seemed. Was it possible to pass through my own neighborhood, a place so densely packed, with the form and cut of my skin so withdrawn that I was not aware of a single soul? Was it the sight of these hags which brought me back? For everyone was there, occupying his familiar place, and they'd been there all along, trying to tear themselves out of the night's brutal jacket. The air was barely breathable, and I thought of the coughing Mildred Osot, and how hard this night must be for her. Aza Luft was there, and Propish the tomato man, along with his wife Gretta, and Marks the candy and nut man, with his two strong boys—all worrying over the conclave of hags under the corner lamp.

Yetta Nostrand, at the door of her little corset shop, wearing a bright cream dress and a pair of white shoes, a trembling sheldrake on an alien lake, was inconsolable at the sight of these women. Her speculations, her threats to call the police, could not be stemmed. She drew around herself Mrs. Costa, the woodworker's wife, and Mrs. Puente, the pregnant wife of Victor Puente, our empty-bottle dealer, and Mrs. Wellerky, who owned the newsstand on Tenth Street. Yetta Nostrand was a small, twiglimbed, superstitious woman. Unmarried, she was rarely given to fits of public emotion. The others now seized on this rarity, expelling advice with compulsive force.

"I want them off this avenue not tonight or tomorrow but right *now!*" Yetta Nostrand began to weep over the menace that she alone saw. "After all, it's here I'm in business and not in Ridgewood—those filthy animals— I want the police!"

Her friends could not in the least placate her. These dirty hags, they were about to lay mayhem on us all. To Yetta Nostrand they were evil jinn. For she was, after all, acrackle with credulity; any straw was an origin, any herring's head her own principality. And quickly she turned blue with hysteria. She bawled and cursed and spun round in her ritual vapors. She took up her newspaper and tore it to bits and let loose a snowfall over all her neighbors' heads . . . to point, by contact and effigy, the approach of certain disaster.

"Goodness, they're not harmin' nothin'," Mrs. Wellerky said. "Yetta, you just can't up and call the cops every time the cat wintches and nobody's causin' no commotion at all!"

"They're a violation, Minna!" Yetta Nostrand said. "I know the law! I was in Judge Merchant's office for ten years, don't you forget it! Look at them!"

"Ah, but they're foul, the foul things," Mrs. Wellerky said. "Yes, a blind man can see how foul they are!"

"A public shame—you mark my words!"

"I think we all ought to lift ourselves up and walk over to Avenue A tomorrow and have a chat with Mr. Ippilito. After all, he's our Republican captain in this neighborhood. Though I hate to show my face in that place. There's always some kind of trouble. We ought to get Esther Cahoon to do the talking, what with her mouth! She can shame a piece of wood red in the face."

Just then, John Helm, attracted by the scene, began to cross the street. He pushed before him the proud little coach which he had artfully spliced for his son out of splinters and bits and fagend chips. The boy, excited by the taut ring in Yetta Nostrand's voice, flopped up and down in his coach, while John Helm tried to calm him. With a wry, clownish smile, the boy cocked his head in an effort to grasp the essence of Yetta's grievance, and he moaned happily. Then I caught sight of it—this high, charging truck. Its weighty mask played out greenish reflections of the corner lamps, headlights frozen with a dead stare, and we all had a premonition of its business. I tried to yell, but was already dumb. The machine sped toward the center of the street, and there it caught them flush, and ground into the pavement forever the little coach, and the wry, clownish smile of the blade-grinder's spastic boy.

John Helm remained with nothing but the handbar in his hands.

In the stillness which followed, there came from the depths of the truck, from beneath the rear wheels, from beneath the pavement, the final crunch of the proud little coach. The truck had rolled several yards and stopped. The driver, a middleaged, orangefaced man with flat features, leaned out of his cab to assess the thing he had struck. He quickly twisted back and slumped over his wheel. He shook, and vomited.

Though the coach was burst open round the dead boy, the boy, miraculously, had escaped even the slightest bruise to his flesh.

Helm fell to his knees at the little body. He would not touch it. The driver's soft continuous weeping was now the lone abiding sound. The heat, which had anaesthetized our senses, lay like a great hand on our heads, pressing us slowly, minute by minute, into the ground from straight above. I remember Helm kneeling quietly, studying the body of his boy, and how lightly he had called out his name—Yutchie—and how the tender melancholy call was choked in the tumid air. I remember too the sudden difficulty I had had in going toward him—my foot would not come easily off the pavement! It sank just a bit when it went forward, and a bit more at each step, and then I could not move it at all. It was as if our streets had boiled for too long into a shallow lake.

But it was true! —I had not invented it! —The pitch-like sublayers had bled up through the cobblestone seams, had risen above the stone surface, had produced a viscid flowing lake of lava. My shoes were already covered, Helm's knees were sunk in it. The truck had furrowed wide, inchdeep tracks in its glutinous wake. There was no footing left for us to move on. And all present had begun to contort between two extremes of terror: the boy's death and the surrender of our city's familiar floor. By now a labored succession of activities was set in motion. We made tentative gestures one way or the other, trying to pull chairs, boxes out of the ooze, trying to retreat into doorways, trying to reach carts and lampposts for leverage and belief, trying, above all, to reach John Helm. We had already begun a puerile howling at each other, delegating the responsibilities away from ourselves for notifying the police, the fire department. The point of dissolution was reached beyond which we dared not step. The mist had thickened, had become the smoking dross coloring the sky, swirling, rolling round us in new amber tones. Here and there—for our neighborhood is vital with speculative energy—a head popped out of a window to investigate the shouting. Gina and Doris Zwar, two sparrows who owned the knitting shop next to Bramovitch, joined hands and managed to reach Yetta Nostrand, and, along with Mrs. Costa, they began a careful wading-out toward the blade-grinder. Behind them, Arab,

Victor Puente's slim Dalmatian, set up a chilling howl.
The poor dog tried to spring after them but the street
had risen to cuff his paws, and he could only lag behind
and howl away his fright. The homeless hags had shrunk
within their own circle to defeat the glob underfoot.
Several embraced. They looked to us to see if this di-
lemma was confined solely to themselves. The old hag,
the old inverted-U hag, whose inversion had fixed her
eyes eternally upon her toes, began to pump her umbrella into the ground, testing her immediate domain
inch by inch. Then she managed to partly untwist herself and look toward John Helm. A cry came out of her
throat, a ripping of wood. The whitewash of her mask
stood out in full relief. Her face was dry, unlike the
others, and her skin was so tightly drawn it might have
been tacked behind her skull. Yet it was a mass of
wrinkles, too. Her mouth was tiny, the skin round it
stitched with hair, and her cry leaped from lips appar-
ently sealed. As though to warn of the menace to vision
in a broken mirror, she raised her umbrella and pointed
it at the bladegrinder. A long thread of tar swung from
its tip. She must have perceived some design in Helm's
sudden flurry of movement. For he had begun to act like
a man ignorant of the presence of death. Rocking back
and forth on his knees, he passed his hands over the little form, describing its outline in the air. He clapped.
He brought his palms together again and again, brought
them to his lips, in a gesture of fulfillment. The little
body had beguiled him. Though it lay now in the street's
ooze, it seemed, at last, to have acquired a fullness denied to it in life. It was no longer a slave to the arbitrary
games of its own nervous system. It was innocent, free
of the demands and brutalities of expression. No more
twisting and contorting, sewing its teeth together with

threads of spit. The grinder's eyes teared as he saw the boy flourish with a new color, a faint, pink tone, a tone of health. No more interior pulling at the young flesh. The fingers were round, robust, and in the little hands and arms not a trace remained of the convulsive angularities of being alive. The boy's honey hair had a new luster. The brow was smooth. The corners of his mouth were lightly turned up in a sad, soft smile. His eyes were halfclosed; a colorless fluid had seeped over the lower lids. Except for a waxysweet porelessness lingering under the fingernails, there was no familiar evidence of death remaining. Helm dabbed with a tricolored handkerchief at the fluid in the boy's eyes. He folded the tricolor and returned it to his pocket. Awash in sweat, he stood now and examined the little corpse. He knelt again and, with a bizarre regulation of motion, as if the problem had but a single, agonizing solution, he picked at and threw aside remnants of the little coach stuck on the boy's clothes. From Fourteenth Street behind him came the undeviating purr of the great generating plant, and then, over this, the grind of a sanitation truck, and, over this, the mournful yawp of a tug from the river two blocks east—and the sounds expired, with no stronger nudge at my balance than one being issued by a random thought.

Worshipfully the grinder worked his right hand beneath the boy's head, and his left beneath his spine, and he gently jogged the body to one side, and let it come back. He did this again before he was satisfied that it would lift out of the shifting pulp with no violence to its newfound poise. He rose up on one knee. He lifted the body and stood; the boy was now cradled in his arms, and I remember the tiny balls of tar stuck on Yutchie's clothes.

He lightly set the loose little corpse on the cycle seat of the grinding cart. He removed his belt; with it he anchored the boy to an eyehook beneath the grinding stones. The small body sagged. With two freeswinging arms the boy went forward, his head striking the large center stone. And then, as if he had immediately seen his rich alternatives, the grinder worked his arm from behind and drew the boy back. He tightened the belt on the eyehook. Under the chin his forearm stayed to prop the small head erect. In sure, consecutive strokes, he adjusted the cycle seat to a proper grinding height. He tapped at a button. Cooling water trickled on the stones. He tapped at a second button. The stones were set flying. From a gunmetal kit he chose a long slender knife and closed the boy's left hand round the grip, and closed his own left hand round the boy's. The tip of the right index he put to the bladepoint, and sustained it there artfully by joining his own fingers into a strong and graceful arch. And slowly the dead boy began to grind his very first blade, learning his craft well and with speed, guiding the blade tenderly across the wet flying stone, swaying softly from side to side, with the rich full pulse of a master behind a masterly wheel of stars.

MONDAY

&rbsp; FIVE MONTHS AFTER THE MURDER OF YUTCHIE HELM, old Cahoon, our janitor, asked me a ritual question: "I hear you've yanked out the bull's horns, Mr. Yago, and decided to join the common herd. Is that right?"

He counted the money.

"Anyway, you're always on time with your rent. More so than most. Ah—have you ever seen a colder Monday mornin', Mr. Yago?"

He went through the dollar bills again, snapping each through his middle finger and thumb. "Faithful," he said. "That counts for a lot."

His kitchen had a window on the court, hidden by a crusted burlap drape. The room was softened by a perpetual dusk. He laughed as he wrote my receipt.

"Sixteen dollars. A turn-of-the-century rent. With rents the way they are today." A true middleman—"Imagine," he said.

A flypaper stalactite, summers old, moved softly in a chill draft. I was impatient. I broached the subject of my rotting door.

"Mr. Cahoon, it's so swollen I can't get it open if it's shut and shut if it's open."

"Some nights I hear you slammin' at it, Mr. Yago. Are you tryin' to slam the world out from under us all? Here in the middle of winter?"

"It ought to be fixed."

"Those doors are a blight to each and every one of us."

"It's been over three years now I've been asking you, Mr. Cahoon."

"F'n the day I set foot in this miserable parcel, a blight, a blight."

"It ought to be fixed."

"Why would you think a man would come in here to take up his life's work? I was struck by a colic in judgment is why. An intestinal congestion of the mind, you might say. And it's been twenty years three weeks this Fridy I suffered the lapse and signed on. And I doubt that I c'n remember a single passin' in and out of a place that was easy, a clear passin' through a portal, you might say. Not a solitary once. We're all in the same boat, Mr. Yago. I might well rent me out for a batterin' ram."

"It ought to be fixed, Mr. Cahoon; there are laws."

"Our landlord is a complicated man."

"So?"

"So more than once he's had the problem. I assure you. Now he sees it, when he sees anythin' at all, this way—it's a question in calculatin' the rottener nut. For me. His agent. In a way. There's pain to me in the price of the fixin', and there's pain to me in the price of the rammin'. One's the stranger, there's no prophesyin' its meanness, the other's a blood relation, already come to terms. Once you get my meaning. —Tell me, do you think we'll have another war, Mr. Yago?"

"We'll have what we deserve."

"Ah—then we'll have the bloodiest war of them all."

Cahoon was a long man, long and dry, an opposite to his wife, who was round and moist. He had a glass eye sparkling in a porous and knotty face. This eye was a mark of pride to him. When he spoke of it, he turned his back on you so that you should also take account of his nape. He had no normal nape, but a three-inch stamp of inlaid skin, a perfect little flag, hairless and purple, which he had received, together with the eye, from Belleau Wood.

"I was stung from behind by a starving Hun," had been his standing explanation. "When I turned to confront the man, his bayonet, a piece of the neck still stuck on the blade, lashed me through the eye. This eye, this bit of neck, they're both buried out at the Wood. The

American Military Cemetray. Though without a headstone to commemorate. Bein' disabled yourself in the line
of duty, Mr. Yago, and though I did my bit of service
some twenty-seven, twenty-eight years before you, I'm
sure you understand my feelin' about leavin' behind a bit
of yourself on foreign soil."

On his head a scurfy black hat perpetually sat. His
hair, like wads of dirty gauze, played out from under its
floppy brim. I'd often seen him, in the presence of a
complaining tenant, especially a Negro, or Puerto Rican,
twist the glass eye from its socket, in full view of the
petitioner, and lay it away in a small flannel sack. The
eye cave he would then lock up with a small denim
patch.

He was a Legionnaire. He was constantly after me to
join his local chapter. I was a choice recruit, he had told
me. The Legion, our country, needed men like me for
proud examples (should he succeed in snaring me his
stature would quickly increase). Despite a generally
humorous approach he had to most issues, I was always
aware of a sour wrath churning in him, bitterblue smoke
in a bottomless jar. He forever gossiped about his wife,
her smoketoned creams and coral cosmetics and lotions
the color of fishscales. "A powerhouse on wheels," he
had told me. "A box of crackerjacks. If you know what
I mean. The woman goes through her life alphabetically,
she's so nervous about her appearance. Oh she's had a
rotten girlhood, I understand that. Myopia, horseteeth,
scaly elbows, et cetera. And pimples, too, big as apples.
But you know, I thought I snapped her out of all that.
Why is it women are such hell on findin' retribution for
their girlhood woes? Whup! . . . phee! . . . a buck
here, two bucks there, and she'll do herself up like a bill-

board. And little Jenny is a piece of the same cake. Christ save her. Marchin' home from school with ink on her chin and wax in her ears when she tries s'damn hard to be like her mother; and all the child wants is a housepet, any sort of furry little thing, which drives her mother mad. Why the kid was cut up somethin' fierce when she stopped at Bramovitch one day and them two kittens a his was layin' dead in the window. Ugliness in a girl, Mr. Yago, is a definite question."

Finally, my receipt signed, he took to contemplating his signature with a lively smile on his face.

"Sixteen dollars. You'll excuse a repetition, Mr. Yago —but a man might do well by offerin' up a candle to the commission on rent controls."

"You know I'm a Jew."

"In my Father's temple there are many houses."

"And what about my door?"

"You're luckier than most men, Mr. Yago. I mean livin' as you do, by yourself. In no danger of bein' crowded out. Now look—I want you to make a mental note of things. You're livin' here, how long? —is it eight years? —well, have I ever taken the liberty to drag you under the skin of things? You profess yourself a storyteller, an observant man. Well, if you can find a bit of leeway, just move round and take stock of an ordinary man's life. This is certainly the kitchen, isn't it? But can you guarantee it? Now take that article there— keep clear of it, the smell is a mutinous thing."

Near his tub was a fake mantelpiece. In eight years, never having had my attention drawn to it, I had never considered its incongruity in the kitchen. On it sat a grimyglass tank full of turtles, each turtle under a pastel shell. Several were dead.

"All I can do, Mr. Yago, is sit like a princely goon on top of this worthless hoard. To say nothing of the aroma."

There was an ancient floor cabinet with various buckets, chipped porcelain on wall shelves, calendars on walls, and an old dented tub for boiling wash under the table, full of potatoes. The table, at which Cahoon now sat, was an oaken wheel set on half a keg. Each chair round it was a wooden box upholstered in wrapping paper.

"Pull apart those curtains, Mr. Yago, if you want to see somethin'. Our parlor, thank you. Mind the curtains, they'll powder in your hands."

Looking into the room, I saw an adjunct of the church.

"Isn't it somethin' to beat all? I'm livin' in a Christmas card."

The Savior bled from walls and windowsills, from chinachests and cupboards, from any spare inch of level surface. I remembered once seeing a wistful, two-inch Jesus perched on the neck of a faucet over his kitchen sink, but it was gone now. Lithographs, images, pictures. The Virgin Bride and assorted Saints. The Child Christ and The Virgin Most Glorious. Most Powerful. Most Renowned. Most Venerable. A carousel of beatific smiles spun round me, flying out like butterflies from every hook and twist.

"You'd best move round like a carpenter's square, Mr. Yago. One wrong move and you'll bring down the whole of Rome. Think of it—at your ear a Ministering Spirit, at your chin an Only Begotten, at your heels a Purifying Host. Come here, son, I want to show you somethin'."

I followed him back into his kitchen. He opened his Kelvinator and pointed.

"I suppose you know my wife's mother is Ukrainian, though Esther herself is Roman through me. The poor girl had to split her loyalties. Look in there, beside that juice container. In time of stress it's the way with Ukrainians."

Between a skyblue pitcher and something I could not recognize stood an earthcolored statuette.

"Mr. Yago, I'd like you to meet the shivering Archangel Pripyat. What d'you think? Look at the way that angel's shoulders are hunched up with the cold. Poor devil. Hungry for intercession and chilled to the chalk. True hypostasis. Ah—you didn't think I was up on my theology, did you? Who does? Old Cahoon the dumb Mick janitor. Eh? Hell, in whose eye does deception dance but the beholder's? You see? In my house all you do is walk in the door to catch yourself in a lie. Two thirds of the Trinity right in that refrig, Mr. Yago— the Archangel Pripyat frosted solid to a block of noodles and cheese."

"I suppose we all have our little weaknesses."

"Don't go on so about your swellin' door with me in this chamber of horrors. Cahoon the dumb Mick janitor. And one day out of every four I've got her mother puttin' up here, too, though she lives just down the street, as you know."

"Yes."

"Ah, well."

Esther Cahoon's mother, Zena Cudcik, was a plate-nosed Ukrainian shank of a woman who spoke not a syllable of English.

"I must admit, Mr. Cahoon, in eight years or so I

don't think I've had half a dozen words with her. I
know nothing of Little Russian."

"Who does? As for myself," he said. "I tried but once
to fathom the roughest Slavic grunt. When Esther and
I were married. The truth is I was bent on findin' out
what in the way of wherewithal the old woman had in
mind for her daughter's dowry. You know the custom
among the old folks. No harm meant. Ah, did we ever
hit it off, we two. Two cows wallowin' around in the
muddy first light of dawn, affectionate enough, mind
you, with a mutual slyness in skirting the other's watering hole."

"And what in the way of wherewithal?"

"The roughest Slavic grunt."

"Hasn't she always been a very poor woman? What
with her becoming widowed just after your wife was
born?"

"I've got no hand in her destiny. There's nobody has
but herself, don't y'know."

"Well, that's as it should be."

"The real truth is, we have a sort of friendship. It all
grows out of this pure dumbness between us. It's a precious thing when you come to think of it. This empti-
ness between us. We've both come to love it too. Now at
the first sign of contact, the very first word, our friendship'll crack and fall into ruin."

"I hope you don't mind an observation, Mr. Cahoon,
but it seems to me that Mrs. Cudcik is not too far from
falling into ruin herself."

"Ah—she's deceived you too! Let me tell you somethin'—in matters of natural law this old lady's perversity
staggers the mind."

"She refuses to die?"

"Refuses? Why, she'll toy round with it just enough

to convince you there's some good in the senile after all.
You've never seen the likes of it. It's all very bad. I'm always wantin' to get a word through to her to find out
just what she has in mind by hangin' on so wild and
fierce."

"She seems warm enough a soul to converse with."

"Ah, but is she warm enough a body? The woman is
a corpse. She's been through every bloody knock save
leprosy. Why, now think, just think when you look at
her. Every blink of an eye is disaster, every ratchety
wheeze is the last. It took me fifteen years to adjust to
her style of pump and bellows. If you'll pardon a turn
on our difference of tongue, she leaves me speechless. If
it's not an arthritic attack one day it's a gallstone rattle
or a migraine roast the next."

"How old is she?"

"Beyond numbers."

Cahoon rose from his chair and arched his back and
produced a dramatic sigh. "She thinks she has half a
chance for immortality. I can't figure any other reason
for it. And yet once a week, and she prefers our meatless
Fridys for such things, she'll heave up, right at the
supper table, a stew full of somethin' resemblin' little
white onions. It's embarrassin', Mr. Yago. It gives you
a few notions on this will-to-survive business."

"What do the doctors say?"

"Hell, the *doctors*. They've been treatin' her over the
years for a grand variety of things. The rampant spiro-
chete, the pussed-up kidney, the defective suppository—
at her age flatulence can be fatal. One clout after another;
a jammed ventricle, an exploding peritoneum, a keeling
vulva—"

"A keeling vulva?"

"They say it's inherited."

Despite his clownish inventory of the old woman's afflictions, and his surprising glibness with physiological terms, it was true that Zena Cudcik had survived through the years a chain of assaults upon her body. Useless, silly, an impediment to her daughter, and suspected of fortunes by her son-in-law, she would bundle in a shawl on Friday mornings, await the mailman for her welfare check, and walk the halfblock east to her children, to spend the rest of the dying day dying. They crouched, her miseries, one inside the other, like a system of Chinese boxes.

When you faced her the noose of asthma tightened before your eyes. And always, out of her throat, would leap a child's cry, by which she meant to prod you into some small remedial tenderness, and her days were split by her cacophonies. Silence would set in later, much later, when there'd be simply no need for it. Meanwhile her fiddlers pumped and her thumpers whacked. In the interests of cold medical logic and Cahoon she should have, many years ago, surrendered, but plague and stubbornness, the material interest and the moral principle, kept beating servility into each other, a battle as old as the earth.

Our inability to communicate through even the simplest words would leave me sorrowful. So, whenever I met her, either on the street, or in our halls, or in Cahoon's apartment, I merely stood and stared. She smelled like a cup of cocoa.

Cahoon thanked me for my rent, in the landlord's name.

"A complicated man," he repeated. "He's cursed with this floatin' eye, y'know. Have you ever run into him, Mr. Yago?"

"No."

"Well, he's cursed with his eye, as I said. He can't keep it quiet. It rolls round and round. I get the feelin' it'll roll right over the bridge of his nose. The man is sensitive about it too. It accounts for his bein' an old-fashioned absentee."

He rose and went to his window to draw aside his crusted drape. We gazed into the court's obscurity. A smoky rain was falling, a city rain, on top of last night's snow. From an upstairs window a radio tinned. The raindrops were large and heavy and made an uneven drumroll on the building wall. Cahoon described several past tenants who came to mind. His reproductions were fastidious. Every cut and bump of a person he summoned up in the telling. And then he turned to me and smiled and pumped my shoulder with a soft hand, proclaiming the pointlessness of all this reminiscence.

He led me to his bedroom.

"Never been in here, have you? Ho! Listen to the jingle of the family bones. Like a bag of bells, eh? Just take a look at that wall, will you? My wife's passion. Bless her. Takes you by surprise, eh? She sees herself an unborn star. She performs on weekends. Big secret. Bet you had no idea. She tells a few jokes, sings, dances. She's got a proper bigtime agent."

On the wall, hanging over a caving brass bed, was a gallery of glossy heads, some smiling, others somber.

"Her colleagues," Cahoon said. "Theatrical people. A nifty bunch, wouldn't you say?"

"I can't quite believe it. I mean, I'm living here a long time and I had no idea."

"You're the first to be in on it, Mr. Yago."

There was something wrong with all the heads, as if they were repelled by the very wall on which they hung. Many were faded, others seemed mischievously scratched. In one a sawtooth line made two of a single nose. Another's right eye was a Christmas seal. Still another had a tack for a tonguetip. They wished Mrs. Cahoon well, with honeydipped smiles, and cast down a baleful moan should truth come out to catcall and spit. There was a desperation on those glossy heads which serviced the passion, and a considerable amount of hair blown wild by the hairsetter's gale. All the heads were inscribed to Evelyn Esther (Esther Cahoon): a great girl, a great singer, our century's finest friend, our country's funniest woman.

"Mr. Yago—you understand this is all sotty voco. I mean, a janitor's wife. The tenants and all. You understand?"

"Perfectly."

"She sleeps with earplugs."

"Your wife?"

"To sharpen her relative pitch."

"Is your wife obsessed?"

"She thinks she's a vision of loveliness."

I tried to imagine her enthralling an audience with her perpetual bosom, her wide flat hands, her special ways. Yet there was something to her face, a sweetness, and her mouth was merciful and frank under a queer spatulate nose. She was a watery talker too, and she moved with definition, as though she was full of right angles.

"The woman thinks she's a grand talent bursting inside."

Cahoon leaned over the bed to flatten a corner curl on one of the pictures.

"Her head fairly teems with endless schemes to put herself before the right people at the right time. With the right amount of clothes left off. I imagine."

"Does she sing well?"

"Like a goat."

"But you said she has a proper bigtime agent."

"Miss Olive Frazee. In the line a ladykingpin. Have you heard of her?"

"No. But you said she sings on weekends, so she must be good enough to hire."

"Sometimes here, sometimes there. Sometimes a big club, sometimes a hole in the ground. It got too hot and close for comfort, but she used to sing over at that little place on Tenth and A. You know it? —Two doors down from that World Council for Slavic Affairs? Where those four big Poles are always sittin' in the doorway?"

"Ah, yes, I know it."

"If you see a Pole by himself, Mr. Yago, it's innocent enough. Two or more in a huddle, they're plottin' a pogrom. That's one of old Bibber's axioms, y'know. Look at that woman's bed, will you?"

On the caving brass bed, riding the eiderdown like drift on an ocean wave, were matchcovers from intimate nightspots, magazine clippings, Hollywood gossip items, congratulatory wires, chewed little tails of dental floss, theater programs, two tin plates for store pies, bills for gowns and makeup, the numberless butts of lipsticked cigarettes.

"She's giving her daughter a proper background."

"Does she have a chance? I mean your wife?"

"The thing is—in that theatrical business they're all such goddam liars. Still and all, when she trowels the grease on good and careful, and fits herself out with a gown to flatter, why, there's somethin' special about her, a *quality*, you might say, and then again she c'n twist this mood into somethin' dirty enough to be a proper spectacle. Forgive me, Mr. Yago—you might think I'm talkin' about a total stranger. But so many years with this thing—I don't know—it's all such a third-rate carnival."

Cahoon and I studied the storage deck of his wife's bed. He was destined to audit her forever, to himself in silence, in whispers to an occasional tenant. On and on he went, threading his eyeless needle. Her bed, his bed, was a huge sump, steaming with the bad breath of unprofitable ambitions. Fifteen years a paltry heap, crushing him down, down.

"Oh, . . . good morning, Mr. Yago."

I turned. Mrs. Esther Cahoon—Evelyn Esther—stood dripping in her kitchen, hugging a wet bag of things to her bosom.

"Off to school with my daughter and up to breakfast with a few hot rolls. Good morning. For ducks, that is. Slush slush slush."

"Ah, sweetheart, . . . I was just showin' Mr. Yago he's not the only soul blessed with a bellyin' ceiling. And tellin' him what a plasterer is askin' these days."

"Good morning, Mrs. Cahoon. I was just in to pay the rent."

She stared at her husband with conventional scorn for guiding me through her untidiness. "You'll pard my gall," she said, "but I think life smells."

Over a slight continuous hiss, she removed her wet things, realigned her poise, and clunked things about with a loud rancorous authority.

"Enough to make a girl heady," she said. "Won't you stay for coffee, Mr. Yago?"

"Of course," Cahoon said. "Of course. Our pleasure."

"You'll pard his manners, Mr. Yago, he's got to be

reminded. A man loses touch with the niceties, being a maintenance engineer."

In the kitchen's perpetual dusk her hair took on the tone of a wet penny. Her eyebrows were indefinite, perhaps reddish. She had forgotten to take off her galoshes and sloshed about unmindful of the noise. Though round and spongy, she had a spirited and compelling way which boxed you in. She was a chain smoker. While she worked, a cigarette kept swerving up to her mouth, and her print dress was cloaked in a lingering vesture of ashes. She smiled at me, according me that bewildered respect of someone who does not quite understand what you are, or what you do.

"Butter or margarine, Mr. Yago?"

"Butter, thank you."

"Oh, this awful city," she said. "And still something else, and still something else. Victor Puente's new baby was bitten by a rat, just this morning too. Have you heard anything, Mr. Yago?"

"No. When did it happen?"

"This morning early is what I heard. They won't take the child to a hospital, being so afraid of not making head nor tails of English. Well, what do the fools expect, not making the least effort? What do we expect, not caring an ounce? Oh, it's the truth, Cahoon, nobody cares, you know that as well n'better than I do."

While she was at the stove, Cahoon winked at me. I was not to consider his wife a mental competitor. He had relinquished all responsibility for her peculiar sentiments.

"Sweetheart," she said to him, "you'd better get yourself down to your precious basement. I saw a few of those dear little hags hopping about your front door."

"You're teasing me, Esther."

"They're cuddled up in your silly ashcans right this minute."

"It'll wait after coffee."

"No, it won't, but suit yourself."

"The thing is, Mr. Yago, I don't mind one or two of them poppin' down out of the weather, but find one you'll find nine. Not that they make a mess, mind you, but they've a genius for springin' my rat traps. Vibrations. I think I'll have to go back to arsenic nuts. You get the notion that women would live with a bit of shame, isn't that right?"

"Those hags are hard to take, I agree."

"Terrible when they're clever. Now you take this Fridy mornin' past. I was down bright n'early to get us a fresh fire goin'. Sure enough, a few, maybe five, maybe six, were bundled up round the furnace and a fire was goin' to burn through hell itself. Now it amused me and I thanked them for their kind assistance. No sooner out of my mouth when one of them, she was a bit cleaner and younger than most, the general run of them—well, she handed me a chocolate bar. Now I bit into the thing and almost lost a few teeth. It was rubber, you see? I laughed out loud, to go along with the situation, and not one of them even chuckled or smiled back. When it was me they made a fool of. And that didn't end it—right away another one sort of chops off a trick thumb and this young one pulls a yard of bloodstained bandage out of her skirts and starts tyin' up the other's mitt. You should've seen this bandage. Red ink, I'll wager. They must've been over to that trick and gadget shop over on Fourth Avenue. I'm still tryin' to reason it out. Their downright *serious*ness, I mean."

"Mr. Yago—have you heard about those kids last

night tearing up that school for the blind down on Rutgers Street?"

"Yes, I did, Mrs. Cahoon. Mrs. Wellerky told me."

"Little butchers."

She put three rolls down in a butter plate and some butter down in a basket. Turning back to her stove, she said: "I prefer tea myself. Go ahead with your coffee. This awful godawful city."

Behind her back, Cahoon patted my shoulder and shushed me emphatically. It was too late. She had already begun to weep. It seemed to've come out of the air. At her stove she grew tall in her grief, as though this was the very first time in her life she'd been honored by tears.

By this unexpected hazard of her emotion Cahoon was deeply embarrassed. He tried a few diversionary clinks with his spoon on the sugarbowl. His wife kept on. The kitchen's dusk was now a tangled skein of designs and resolves for which there were no antidotes.

"Dear Esther—you have greatness, believe me."

Behind her girlish sobs he motioned me closer.

"One must allow a dead woman her delusions," he whispered.

Mrs. Cahoon edged toward her bedroom. Unwilling to expose the gruel of her makeup, she kept her face to the wall. She faded behind the curtains.

Cahoon went on, whispering: "It'd be nothing but vicious to strip her delusions away. I've not done the finest job providing, after all. Y'know, Mr. Yago—it's only through these delusions that a dead woman'll consent to think of us at all. Don't you agree?"

"I don't understand a word of that."

"Think about it—what is it all about, after all? Scuffin' for the buck, dead mornin's and deader nights, a few hot meals, a glass of beer, a little romancin', a few kisses, a movie, some heartburn, rent to pay, two new songs and an old suit, a little froth and sparkle, and you have it. History. Life. Why they're nothin' but all these delusions laid end to end which the dead entertain for the living. A continuum, y'might say. The past for the present. Ah, listen—she's in there now replasterin'. Bless her. Sorry about this little domestic scene. And it's true, y'know—great holy empires, wars, little joys, big tears, everythin', everythin', why they're nothin' but the little bits of magic the dead consent to spin for us. Well—in a word, why blame the dead?"

"You'll have to be clearer, Mr. Cahoon."

"My friend, the dead give us somethin' to start out with."

With my spoon I began scraping at crumbs. Puttering about and jarcap sounds replaced the sobs from the bedroom. Cahoon patted my hand.

"My estimates of her talents are by no means exaggerated."

"If she's dedicated, Mr. Cahoon, I think you must take her seriously."

"Oh, I assure you, I assure you."

"I don't mean to be presumptuous, but maybe another child."

"But she *can't*. Didn't you know our little Jenny is here on a foster arrangement? Poor Esther—she's a blank inside when it comes to that. You and I—we'll never know the bitterness of the bald vine that dies of a winter to stay dead forevermore. Not that little Jenny hasn't helped. But not enough, not enough. There's half the reason for my wife stormin' about so. Little Jenny was dumped at birth on the loadin' ramp of that old bottlin' plant down on Madison Street. And her first

foster parents, why, they booted her out when profits
from the arrangement began to lag. A child's growin'
appetite too much overhead. Imagine. Pleasant people,
eh? Well, we've got her now, with God's help, and an
adoption in the works. By the way, Mr. Yago, I hear
you're lookin' round for a job. Have you given up on
the storytellin'?"

"No. It's just that it's a little tough to live on my pension these days."

"And what does that come to, if you don't mind?"

"A hundred and thirty-eight dollars a month."

"I've got a little proposition to put to you. Ah, not
now—here she comes—shhhh—"

Having worked very hard, Mrs. Cahoon brought herself back to life. She came in to us rather proudly. She
poured tea and sat.

"More coffee?" she asked of me.

"Thank you, no."

"A glass of tea and suck?" Cahoon said.

"No, I'm fine."

"Dear Esther, I was just tellin' Mr. Yago that you have
an appealin' stagecraft. One that bears watchin'."

"Yes, Mrs. Cahoon. It sounds exciting."

"But you have, you *have,* dear. Why crinkle up your
nose? You've a lively flair for pantomime."

"I won't bring my daughter up in this slaughterhouse.
This godawful city. I won't."

"Dear, haven't I always told you to get your ideas
down in writing?"

Too devious for a pointblank show of disgust, Cahoon, with solemnity, began to stir nothing in his empty
cup. Mrs. Cahoon, built up in three tiers of first-come
sales, and a utility-minded look in her eyes, began, with
a curious mumble, to give her kitchen a going-over. Her

mumbling grew louder, more indistinct, as she appraised the chalk and splinters of her handiwork.

"Chupyeh," she said.

"Beg pardon?" I said.

"Chupyeh chupyeh."

"Aha—wonderful," Cahoon said.

Her mumbling, then, took on a pulse of its own, and dressed itself in a song:

> *". . . chupyeh chupyeh sheke retchke*
> *naptypyeh zheshnoche*
> *yezhelimee nyevyezitche*
> *pura huvotch kustche. . . ."*

"Aha, adorable," Cahoon said. "If you chop a tree with an axe, Mr. Yago, while reciting this little ditty, you'll finish up with sixteen chops every time. Adorable. An old Polish neighbor taught her that. She's dead now, poor woman. Must be ten years. Hemorrhaged in bed and lay in her own cold waters for near three days. Then it started seepin' through on the people underneath. It's a happy thing she didn't have any sort of linoleum on the floor—or the poor woman might be layin' up there yet. Dear, why don't you try your new sketch out on Mr. Yago?"

"No."

"It's so good—I mean it's an opportunity."

"No."

"She's a bit shy. Do you remember Yutchie Helm— the bladegrinder's boy—and how he was killed last summer?"

"I was there when it happened."

"Ah well. Y'see it inspired Esther to a sort of little somethin'. How can I put it plain? She takes the part of two mediums—you know the sort—it's a sort of ridicule, and somehow, one not knowin' what the other's up to, these two characters contact the same noisy little poltergeist for their respective clients. They naturally run head-on way out in the never-never. Now you c'n imagine the brawl over jurisdiction, and they take it into the courts. It's a regular circus, Mr. Yago."

"I wonder how my mother is getting on?" Mrs. Cahoon said.

Cahoon shrugged.

"I'd better get me down to the basement and rout the hags out. Y'know—they're beginnin' to get a taste for this building."

He weaved his way toward the door, careful in the extreme to keep from brushing against the clutter.

"Good mornin', Mr. Yago, I'll see the landlord hears about your door. Drop in soon again."

He blew a kiss to his wife and winked at me.

He had mentioned a "proposition." It was merely a hint. By dropping it so abruptly I knew that he meant to be pursued.

"Don't you believe a word of it," Mrs. Cahoon said. "Between your door and the landlord my husband stands like a telephone pole. You can bet on that. —Nor about those awful, awful creatures. He charges them all a bit of rent, did y'know that? Oh, yes. Our dear little jellyeyed landlord isn't on to half of Cahoon's carrying on. My husband's running himself a proper little hotel downstairs. A quarter a night, I think it is he charges. And no questions asked about luggage."

"That's hard to believe. I mean there are laws, Mrs. Cahoon."

"Mr. Yago," she said, and closed her eyes to dramatize my essential defectiveness of the mind, "what does the law mean to an Irish Catholic turned New York? Who hasn't been to a Mass maybe but twice in his life."

"He was born on the other side?"

"Tumbled out of steerage, the dear sweet man, when he was nine years old. And naturalized on his father's papers."

"I didn't know that—"

"Oh, I don't know any more. The only thing he's affectionate about are those Sunday soccer games up at Randall's Island. Must be something of the brute in him that has a taste for that silly game. Do you think so?"

"Well, it's a game, Mrs. Cahoon—"

"He'll die as he lived, that man, in his own silliness. It's not that he's stupid. He's quite an educated man, you know."

She became quiet and thoughtful. What did she wish with me? She sipped at her tea and protested kittenishly. "Oh, I've made it too sweet again!"

All at once her anxiety over the appearance of her rooms erupted into a barrage of apologies. She dusted and rearranged. My appeasements did little to quiet her.

"You don't have to bother, Mrs. Cahoon. I was just leaving."

Businesslike, though intensely social, she talked about war, the city, prices, old songs, actors, and, ultimately, diets. An expert on food and figures, she laid out a monthlong menu for me. Her words snapped out of her mouth in their own swift fashion, so swiftly they would not honor rights of position or precedence, snapping out into the kitchen's perpetual dusk and crashing in a pileup of verbs and adjectives. Now and then she became a most earnest inquisitor into human behavior, shooting out vast questions concerned with motive and meaning.

"Oh we've given up—but why is it the fear of another war?—why look at us in this skinless place—we're a cheerless lot—a darling bunch—and belong in an older world —you know Europe—maybe once we put up a fine front when people cared and took pains to dab a bit of polish and paint now and then—I can't forget my young ladyhood—and the city was so sweet."

Windblown and depleted, she sat again at the table. Forgetting herself, she put the dustcloth to her nose. Through it all she did her best to appear a wicked little bag of tricks.

She stood and backed against the only clear space of wall, as if to mount it like a piece of calender art. And from the wall, she gossiped and pried and wheedled, trying also to remain quite proper and businesslike.

"It's just that he has no desire to up*lift* himself," she said, stepping down off the wall.

She was born to defeat. Her life he had snapped like a grackle bone, had forgotten it on the windowsill, till an army of ants had brought it martyrdom. Whenever he emerged from his cellar there was a new blue bump on his face from something or other. She was sick and tired of his garbage cans, his stock of fuses. Sick of the disfigured little pictures popping out of his mouth concerning their future. God for a hot busting belly, a belly so hot it would char the touch! His incurable colitis! His unbelievable mouth! She was a pitiful wreck beset by both ends of an egomaniac.

"I've got the makings of a solitary drunk, Mr. Yago, just you wait and see."

She tapped her finger on the teabag canister, announcing her death by boredom.

"So he let the cat out of the bag. Would you really like to see me perform?"

"Oh, yes, Mrs. Cahoon, oh, yes."

"Not that awful thing about the mediums—that's *his* taste in things. If you know what I mean. Heavens. I think I will. Now you sit over there."

She directed me to a small bench covered by a green oilcloth and crisscrossed by rope. Lower than the kitchen table, I strained my neck viewing the imaginary stage. She stepped into her bedroom. From there, I was asked to busy myself with my thoughts. I wondered about Cahoon's "proposition."

She poked her head between the curtains, reappeared entirely, dressed in a full headdress of feathers brightly colored, a buckskin costume, and redbeaded sandals. She clicked the light switch on and off, to start her sorcery. She did this so cleverly she seemed to emerge from a red, red sea. She stepped toward me and, with a deep breath, halted with perfection, and gestured to the orchestra in her mind's pit and cocked her head to the overture. As round as she was, she stood straight up and down, her arms flat to her sides, rising, rising, as if to shoot up to the ceiling. Subtly, she pouted, to confirm my captivity. I began to applaud, but her eyes were forlorn. My applause grew louder, and louder, and then, before my eyes, she solidified into a rising block of wood. I marveled at her control.

"Mrs. Cahoon, that's brilliant! I know what you're doing! You're a wooden Indian coming to life—you're pushing back time, no frontiers for you—it's an authentic piece of Americana!"

"Can you imitate a tomtom?"

"Let me try."

She handed me a hatbox with a beaded chain. I began to drum.

Just then, somewhere in her, or on her, a movement. Implicit. Explicit. Barely discernible. Then another. She broke down, ever so slowly, into distinct segments of activity, actually breathing life into a lifesized block of wood. I drummed. I punted my toe on a table leg and punctuated her creation with suitable whacks on my tom-tom.

A knuckle twitched, a muscle moved, an eye flicked, a finger hutched, a leg kicked, an arm shot out in a spasm.

And, after a slight, witty intimation of a war dance, she wheeled to face me as if in sudden affray, and she let out the lowest moan a human throat can produce.

"Look at me! . . . look at me! . . . am I so vile? . . . so low? . . . am I without a soul? . . . am I just a thankless plank to whittle on? . . ."

BAM, I went on my tomtom, FLOOSH BAM WHUMP WHUMP WHACK.

"Oh look at me! . . . No rage am I from the Osage
                        Unspoken by Spokane.
                        The Erie, Seneca, or Naskapi
                        Disclaim my stamping by a
                           pappy.
                        Just look at me! . . . Do you see?
                        A heart that's never understood
                        And all because it throbs in
                           wood?"

BAM BAM WHUMP WHUMP BAM

                        ". . . Nor Minnie from the Seminole
                        Nor Alice from Algonquin.
                        A Sioux, a Ute, a Crow, a Cree

Defies my claim to family tree.
Just look at me! . . . Do you see?
A heart that's never understood
And all because it throbs in
       wood?"

"Beautiful, Mrs. Cahoon—beautiful!"

With a whip of the wrist her toy tomahawk scalped a
hundred heads. She defended her bloodletting with
smiles so sweet that to be her victim was glory enough.
So tender, so full of humanity, so melancholy over the
fate of her beloved wooden Indian.

BAM WHUMP BAM BAM WHACK. BAM BAM
                    ". . . They're all of them beyond my
                         ken
                    Susquehanna and Cheyenne,
                    Shawnee, Pawnee, Huron, Oto,
                    Modoc, Chinook and Papago,
                    The Pueblo, the Nootka, the
                         fiery Mingo,
                    One and all debase my lingo.
                    Just look at me! . . . Do you
                         see?
                    A soul in hell which thirsts for
                         good
                    A spirit in darkness which shivers
                         in wood?"
CRACK BAM FLOOSH BAM BAM

Her song went on and on about its mournful business
. . . where to run when her song was done? What to
chase? Though she danced her dance through wooden
chambers, wasn't she one with us? Isn't it love, only love

which matters? Love popping out from under a cup,
from behind a page, from under the wing of a moth?
Must we be forever appalled at our dry mornings, our
galloping nights? Is it love which tells us who we
are? . . .

She finished. Then, nodding to me, she faded behind
her curtains, indicating, with a soft smile, it was proper
now to applaud.

"You're too kind," she said on coming back.

"It was pure enchantment, Mrs. Cahoon."

"You did very well on the tomtom."

"I was under the influence, Mrs. Cahoon. I was swept
along."

"You're too kind," she said again. "You'll pard me,
but I've got to do myself up in a few ribbons and rags.
The DSC'll be along any minute and our cans aren't
even up on the sidewalk."

In the matter of lighting our halls, Cahoon's ethic,
proceeding directly from his mysterious link with the
landlord, was clear and unyielding. Over each landing
hung a five-watt bulb. Each bulb, having long endured,
had a hairyblack bark of flywings and sludge. Our halls,
the narrowest on our street, had a coalshaft's illumination.

During the day, coming from nowhere, and at night,
coming from our five-watt bulbs least of all, our light
was a bastard light, of no time and no place. It was
sourceless and ancient, mystifying and changeless. As
guilt. All things passing through it were toned by special
drama; my neighbors were organic sprouts, murky and
faceless, submitting to no other end but an end to themselves. Our walls sagged along the edge of the world.
They would sweat in the bitterest cold. They smelled

of vinegar and manure. Our steps were a century's patchwork, with a dull flatfurry coat, as if they'd been rugged
by rathide.

Each landing was a scrapdealer's loft, a regular
Broome Street beehive, glutted with city junk. Under
the load our stairs leaned away from the vertical. On
the landings were lanes and avenues to be lost in, arches
to march through, labyrinths changing through a com-
post of history: incredible things, jigs and jags and brica-
brac, findings and remnants, statuary and sticks, and
out of some hidden era there always floated the mingled
fumes of wild mint and cabbage, of St. John's bread and
roofer's pitch, of alcohol and catpiss.

Here and there beside a blistering door sprouted an
artificial plant and, as you climbed the stairs, a brittle
glume or spikelet cracked underfoot to refine the il-
lusion somewhat. Bunchings of sighs and laughter, sad,
mocking, seductive, leaped from under a junkpile hat,
from behind a charred diploma. When it rained there
was no end to the crescendo winds whipping at the
bones of our tenement, veering through Cahoon's light,
spraying up our noses the residual silt of our giant New
York.

FRIDAY PREVIOUS

℘ BIBBER HAD CONCLUDED IN HIS DEEPEST HEART THAT
his cousin would hire me. Baron, the cousin, owned an
ironworks plant in Brooklyn.

On the strength of a letter, which had taken him four days to compose, in which, under a tide of hyperbole, I was portrayed as a Brobdingnagian of heroism, of decency and responsibility, Bibber had decided that my meeting with his cousin was in essence superfluous, a gesture, and that his own signature, at the end of those wonderful lines, was tantamount to Baron's signature at the bottom of my first paycheck.

The letter had preceded me into Baron's office by two days. I did not know it existed. Baron waved it under my nose as an afterthought—the way, on occasion, a burning ambition will follow an arbitrary success.

The morning was cold, alive with sunlight. The wind put a golden bite on the cheek. Baron's plant was on Flushing Avenue, four blocks beyond the Navy's Receiving Station. Long sections of old car track still ran to the bridge approach. The avenue itself was a mottle of cobble and asphalt. Over it electrified buses ran. The Navy Yard induced a feeling of activity and significant events, yet the whole neighborhood suffered a lingering gall of neglect. It made no sense in a morning so sharp and alive. Blankfaced buildings lined street after street, with not a trace of color in all the wooden dullness. The bright morning sat on these framework blanks like a sarcasm. Each structure was on a tilt—so fragile, in fact, that the momentary grace of a roof-perched wren would prove insupportable. Here and there an out-of-the-way business made a quiet stand for survival: an exterminator, a notions store, a petless pet shop.

On every corner, brooding at the Navy Yard walls, was a saloon dark and obscure, and weak with structural rickets. A profound lassitude issued from its windows, where a sign proclaimed some long-forgotten neighborhood dance, a double feature in a local movie-house now defunct, a Congressional candidate, who still smiled weakly for his ghostly electorate.

Baron's plant shared the block with a warehouse for fine imported veneers. Both low buildings were attached, identical. Formerly they were car barns, standing at the juncture of three abandoned trolley lines. Each weather wall had two bell windows with broad stone sills. The sills were pocked with craters, the windows heavily masked by deformed bars. Once the buildings were painted entirely black, now they were simply dark.

On the walk, near a green wastebin flush to the wall, was an oildrum on steelstrap legs, with draftholes at the bottom. A low fire burned. The oildrum smoked.

Two highsliding doors were slightly parted. I went in. The place was a frozen hollow. Cumbersome bulks and angles were in constant movement. My eyes were flashed by spasms of welding light. Tall canlike heads with single window-eyes kept dipping into the cruel spasms of light. A flat sheet of buttoned steel floated over the workers' heads. It rode via cable under a crisscross ceiling track while a man tugged a freefloating pulley. Going through an aisle between millstock walls of steel, I came to a man sitting on a puncher. He was playing with a glove and yelling to a nearby man who, unresponding, slapped redlead with a soft brush along a fabricated column on a pair of old iron horses.

Behind the gross puncher a man tonged glowing rivets out of a heater. Rythmically, in a graceful little dance, he tonged the steepleheads, swinging from the heater to an I-beam, putting the rivets through. Opposing him across the beam another man waited and bucked, waited and bucked. Throughout they carried on a dialogue inaudible to me, and, I think, even to themselves.

The noise in Baron's place was worse than any I had heard in combat.

The man at the redlead bucket swung his brush toward a dirty glass cubicle, showing me where Baron might be found. The flat buttoned sheet returned, like a geometric cloud, passing over my head. As I ducked, the pulley man smiled. He drew two fingers across his throat, symbolizing my eventual decapitation.

The light in this plant was no better than Cahoon's light. To untried eyes any work seemed impossible, yet calipers walked over blueprints, and level bubbles hovered over angle frames, and a variety of gates and rails twisted hotly into ornamental whimsies.

The toggle bucks made the most noise of all. Here and there sparks flew, or poured, like grain to the floor. The noise had become my black beast.

Baron was not in his glass cubicle. I sat on a rivet keg near his desk and waited. A young man in paintcrusted coveralls walked in. He carried a cakebox filled with coffee containers and he set one on Baron's desk.

"I'm looking for Mr. Baron," I said.

He smiled, and produced a conspiratorial wink. I followed him into the plant and through an orange arch and down a steel stairwell with nodular steps. I was glad to be away from the noise, though the steps were charged with vibrations. ZoooOOOP . . . zoooOOOP . . . zoooOOOP. . . .

"What's that?"

"The boss. On his magic carpet," the young man said. Once more the conspirator's wink, and the mischievous smile. He ran back up the stairs.

This subterranean vault was spacious, though the light was as bad as the light upstairs. The filtered noise from above emphasized its strange, inactive character. There was nothing here: that is, nothing that I could discern offhand. I stood at the base of the stairwell, feeling as if a joke had been played on me. My willow limb does not take kindly to stairs. My pelvic harness had begun to pinch. But my vow to see the situation through to the end had had the solemnity of a covenant sealed in blood. Into this very moment my friend Bibber had poured a good deal of passion. His passion had precluded any possible error in judgment. His cousin owned an ironworks. I needed a job. Hence the deed accomplished.

ZoooOOOP . . . zoooOOOP . . . zoooOOOP. . . .

From somewhere beyond a low cinderblock wall, at the furthest reach of this underground vault, an ingenious little cab came sailing through the air. In it Baron sat, closed round by a transparent shield. So this was his magic carpet. It rested in the bend of an otherwise vertical steel member, like a ball in a jai-alai wicker. The steel member rode a network of ceiling tracks similar to the one upstairs. It had a swivel suspension. Movement within movement. It had an exhilarating, gyroscopic freedom. And it flew along swiftly, with a high crescendo sound, while the cab slowly revolved. Fifteen feet up, Baron had a full field of vision.

The cab halted over my head. I walked toward the stairwell until I could see the man inside. He stuck his head over the shield.

"You see a kid with coffee?"

"Yes . . . he's upstairs."

"The dummy."

"Mr. Baron?"

"I see salesmen Thursday mornings."

"I'm not a salesman. My name is Yago. Barney Yago."

"Who?"

"Barney Yago. Your cousin Bibber—"

"Oh *you're* the guy. I didn't expect you so soon. Matter of fact, I got his letter right here—"

"Letter?"

"Would you like a ride, Mr. Yago?"

"Can you spare a minute, Mr. Baron? I've been here near half an hour."

"I've been here near thirty years. What's your rush? Hold on . . . what's the name? Yago? Nice name. Watch it now, watch it."

The vertical member shivered. It began to lengthen downward, one beam sliding through another. The cab came down.

"Some setup, eh? This is a twelve-twenty eight riding on wheelbearings inside a fourteen-inch sleeve."

The cab sat down on a rubbernosed spike which finally touched the floor. "You know what I'm talking about?"

"No," I said.

"That's what I figured."

The shield half of the globe flapped over and he stepped out. We shook hands. He had a thick gloomy air about him. "That's what I figured," he said again. "Bibber never heard of a union. I'm running a school for willing youngsters. You're not such a young youngster at that. So. What are you—some postgraduate *yeshiva bucher* of his?"

"I'm his next-door neighbor."

"You know, this is the way my cousin Bibber keeps in touch. He sends me applicants for jobs. You're a postcard between relatives, Mr. Yago."

"Did you say something about a letter, Mr. Baron?"

"He wrote me."

"I didn't know that."

"Well, you're the boy who beat Hitler singlehanded. You've got a Silver Star, with two clusters, a DSC, no family except for an older sister, a 1947 Oldsmobile the government gave you gratis, a desire to write, a wooden leg, a head for figures, a pension for life, courage like a tiger, a collection of books which amazes even my cousin, a passion for neatness, an ear for languages, a wonderful eyesight, an honesty which will keep you broke the rest of your life, the best of health, no love for drinking, terrific teeth, a respect for authority. What have you got in the line of steel fabrication?"

"I think Bibber thought something in the office."

"You a bookkeeper?"

"No."

"Take shorthand? File?"

"No."

"If you're a writer are you a *tech*nical writer?"

"No."

"Can you read a blueprint?"

"Before the war I did some ink tracing."

"On what? For whom?"

"Marine boilers. Refinery installations. The Foster-Wheeler Corporation."

"What's a section?"

"A section of what?"

"A section. What's an elevation? What's an isometric projection?"

"Mr. Baron, I think we're wasting each other's time."

"Where's the tiger's courage? Do my questions embarrass you?"

His mouth was alive with bridgework. From between the flattest lips a mobile, sharp, gold construction con-

tinually rode out, then snapped from sight almost instantly, in the manner of a turtle's head under attack.
Except for this, everything about him was gloomy and
broad.

Through a plain face, over which a smile fitted like a
glove on backward, his words tumbled out one on top
of the other, in a fierce pursuit of that turtle's head. His
head was a pink dome, coped by a few filaments of
hair. Like a man working in the wind, his eyes were
trapped in water, as though the water had been piped
into the sockets through two sandy pouches that swung
on his cheeks. His coveralls were so small he was unable to bend or pivot or raise his arms. He shook my
hand with robot mobility.

I was confused by his gloom. These quick punitive
questions—was he conversing with Bibber through me?
It was plain that he did not believe I'd been in ignorance
of Bibber's letter, which had begun to resemble Swin-
burne's absurd tribute to Victor Hugo.

Then, he said: "Ah, these guys, these guys."

He walked away from me, stuffing his work gloves
into a back pocket. He sat on a step in the steel stairwell
and lit a cigarette. I remained at the cab. His mood had
changed. He looked at me and shrugged, in a benign
way. He motioned me to sit on an unopened rivet keg
nearby. I refused.

"Let me tell you about the last fellow Bibber sent me."

"Look, Mr. Baron—you don't have to explain."

"Can't you hold your horses? Who's coming to who
for what? You're supposed to be a writer. I'm not such
a *bulvon,* my friend, be careful. Doesn't the question of
relationships concern you?"

This last remark astonished me. He stopped talking.
He selected a nodule on a steel step and ground his

cigarette into it with a flourish, to punctuate the sequence of ideas just transmitted. He began to whistle, and pull a glove back on.

A thin sound, a hiss of steam, from I did not know where, sprang up.

"Now he's fired the boiler. *Now!*" Baron said.

I had begun to feel the power-thick dust of this underground vault. It lay on my lips and my mouth was dry. My fingers were dry as matchsticks and would easily ignite. The thick powder covered everything: the steel steps, Baron's pink dome, the globe of his airgoing cab, the overhead tracks, the silver meters on the walls, the odds and ends that'd been stored for years, the broken machines, the few legless chairs, the engine block ablaze with rust.

He stood up and began to pace back and forth. Putting his gloved hands behind him, he began to speak again in quiet flat tones.

"My friend, nature's pulled a fast one. You take my cousin Bibber. He's bloated with righteousness, fat as a melon with his wornout *ethical* way to deal with life. But what about the *real* Bibber? What about the real *you?* Will I ever get to know you? Not on your life. Even if we slept together for twenty years the only thing I'll get to know about you is that you're younger than I am. Do you know what youth is? Panic and arrogance. That's all we ever get to know about being young. Panic and arrogance. Which is nothing. That's why we're helpless. Me, you, Bibber, the morons upstairs with their stupid unions, the whole city. We're know-nothings. I have a fine wife and three fine children and my beautiful house teems with living and the truth is I live with four helpless ghosts in a temple of silence. You know my wife as well as I do, and you don't even know her first name. That's nature's scheme for helping people get along with each other. Listen, my friend, I'm on a first-name basis with the biggest of the biggest in this city, and do you know what success is? A performance, an act, and death is the audience. It's true, it's true."

As he spoke, as one idea fertilized another, I realized that the original purpose of my meeting with him was lost forever.

"The young, the young," he said, "The privilege of the young: to hell with everything that isn't youthful. That's the most that can be said about being young—panic and arrogance. That's why, buddy, there's nothing hard in making wars, in sending the young out to butcher each other. In peace they're ignored, so they'll manage it on their own. Look at *you*—you come to a place like this for a job. You. A man with one leg. For Christ's sake, you have to be a mule to even walk *out* of here at the end of a day's work. You want to des*troy* yourself? I'm not asking you to hold up your wooden leg like a dripping fish to remind yourself; but, my God, a little pro*portion*. Bibber and his young men. Where does he find them? Don't be insulted, I'm only talking. What I mean is, you and I, in this situation, cannot be two diplomats wearing spats and chinking at a bottle of wine with our fingernails. A couple of weeks ago he sent me another young man. So intense, so brilliant. Ah, what a meatball! All right—let's forget his experience around an ironworks. He gave me his name and there was nothing else to talk about. So I asked him what he be*lieved* in. 'I believe we're lost,' he tells me. 'Lost?' I said. 'Who?' 'Oh, we're all lost,' he said. 'Who? Who?' I kept asking. 'You and I,' he said. 'The French, the Russians, the English, the Democrats, the Republicans, the Communists, the Baptists, the Jews, the Catholics, the scientists, the poets, the fairies, all of us.' 'How can you live?' I asked him. 'Why don't you hang yourself?' 'I'm lost,' he tells me. 'Lost is blind. Suicide is solution. That's our tragedy. We're blind, condemned to an eternal inability to see any solutions.' Have you ever heard of such a moron? Such garbage? And mind you, to a potential employer? The worst thing is, he's probably right. That highminded silly son of a bitch is probably right. Did he ever give me looks when I laughed in his face. Come on, Mr. Yago—take a ride with me. What can you lose? I want to show you something—"

I tried to explain that, due to my limb, I would be unable to climb into the cab with him. His soliloquy left me sad, gross, and vulnerable. I wanted to get out of his plant. He smiled. He persisted, with something pathetic in his invitation. Then, getting into his cab, he said: "Hey—you want to hear something?"

Before I could answer, he cupped his hands round his mouth and quickly, uninhibitedly, he reproduced the sounds of batwings and sirens. Of sleds on asphalt and Donald Duck. Of crashing clouds and butter churns and dogs in heat. He was remarkable. "Wait!—Wait!— What's *this* one?" And out they came, the fissss of a Roman candle, a fingernail on glass, the turning of a page, a dentist's drill, a tin can rolling down the street.

"Come on—come on, Yago, get in! Get in! Oh, come on!—"

Was he mad? I don't know, but there was something of Bibber's smoldering in the man. I allowed myself to be crowded into his contraption. Once in the cab, the transparent shield up before us, once up in the air so gossamer and weightless and vibrating along, he talked to

me as though he was the only being on earth to whom
I'd given the privilege of intimacy.

"And don't tell me what you go through," he said. "I
know. I know. Tell me, Yago, is there anybody in the
world who has seen you undressed with your leg on,
except for a few nameless whores? Of course not! . . .
But I know what it is. The flashy shoe and the argyle
sock on the bald wooden leg. Hah! . . . That flesh-
tinted shell! Admit it, Yago. It's a piece of idiocy that is
not even a poor duplication of the thigh. Come on, Yago
—admit it!"

I told him to stop. I told him to descend, to let me
out. But he went on, and, in a moment, with startling
accuracy, he mimicked the creaks and clanks and leather
squeaks of my willow limb on the walk, the soft com-
plaints of my pelvic harness. "What can I tell you?" he
said. "What can I tell you, buddy? But, Yago, think of
your advantages! Think! You've got only five toenails
to trim. *Five!* And only one leg to stumble on. One lucky
leg to defend against the common scourges!"

"For the love of God, Mr. Baron, cut it out!"

"The common scourges, Yago! —The mosquito bites
and athlete's feet, the bunions and trench feet, the corns
and charley horses, the scales and instep ridges, the in-
grown toenails and varicose veins and blistered heels
and all the miserable cancers!"

I screamed at him. He quit. Here, crowded with him
in this absurd contraption, suspended over a shivering
jumble of small wooden crates, I was trapped.

He began to hum, and chuckle! Then, he offered me
his hand.

"Yago! —I'm fed up with people who take me the
wrong way. I understand about the little walls to crouch

behind. Right? You know what throws *me,* personally? The bomb. You see this little gimmick we're riding round in?—I'm crouching. Buddy, this is where I spend my working day. I haven't seen the sun in ten years. Look down over there, behind those acetylene tanks— look at those doors, buddy. Wait, now . . . now you can see them."

Beyond the low cinderblock partition, in an area which seemed more brightly lit, there stretched along three walls an endless procession of doors. Baron halted the cab so that I could see them all at once.

"My love. My vice. My life," he said. "In the last ten years there hasn't been a building torn down in this city which is not represented by at least one door in this collection. Just look at those doors, will you? Buddy— they prove we once had a civilization in this city. Look at them all, huh? The woop and warf of New York."

"You mean the woof and warp."

"Who would think it, such masterpieces in a brute of a city like this?"

And slowly Baron gave motion to our little cab, and the doors marched by in an endless parade. I could not believe my eyes. There were doors of every sort: slab, flap and leaf doors; double, single, and folding doors; groove, stile, and rail doors; of basalt and bronze; of cedar, oak, and cyprus; of dolorite and elm. There were silver and brass doors to bring tears to Homer's eyes, and olivewood for Solomon. However they were, tenoned or hinged, there were doors to swing at the Baptistry of Florence and marvels of metalwork for Notre Dame. Figured and foliaged, carved with the egg and the tongue, bas-reliefed and landscaped, Gothically niched, classically pilastered, there were doors in that endless parade that might have made Michelangelo envious. At the head of each group of doors was a placard on a long stick which identified the locale where each was found. Richmond Hills, Bensonhurst, Sutton Place, Pelham, Highbridge, Washington Heights, Kips Bay—

He repeated, with a festive ring in his voice, his first-name connection with the city's big men, clarifying his tie-in with certain demolition contractors, and how it gave him first crack at the doors when a building came down. Every month he would have his doors carried outdoors and cleaned. The men welcomed a break from the routine above, but they were pallbearers carrying corpses to be washed down. Listening to him, seeing his doors, I was filled with an unpleasant premonition, yet I was fascinated. Baron spoke of our streets, of our city.

"It's a plague, don't you see?" he said. "A plague. Ah, it's an orgy, it's always been with us, this stripping away, this bowel movement. Look how we tear down in the name of—"

"I'm getting a little nauseous up here, Mr. Baron. This thing is beginning to swing. Couldn't we go down?"

"Thattaboy—extend yourself," he said. And then, he pulled out Bibber's letter and waved it under my nose and tore it into bits and tossed it into the air while the cab went down.

"It was nice of you to drop by, Mr. Yago. Please relate my thanks to Bibber. Tell him I'm sorry we could not work things out."

Going up the stairwell into the main plant I heard the zoooOOOP . . . zoooOOOP of Baron's magic carpet.

TUESDAY

ᘒ AFTER CAHOON'S WIFE HAD PRESENTED ME HER
wooden Indian, I went to bed. When I woke I found
the day gone. I realized that I had missed an appoint-
ment at the limbfitters. I dressed and went next door to
Bibber. He was not yet home. So I went down and out
into the neighborhood to look for him.

It was past midnight when I reached home. Arab,
Victor Puente's swift Dalmatian, skulked and slid over
the glazed streets, enriching Szold Place with a track of
steaming coins. Four windows were lighted in two
woodworking lofts opposite our building. In one doorway an old hag was asleep on her cardboard slab. Near
her a battered, babyless carriage was filled with forty
cents worth of trashcan ferreting. Her nightcap was a
woman's stocking, her pillow two dry wrists locked by
the weight of her head, her quilt a square of awning
with flagwide stripes and a faded legend: NEW WORLD
RELIGIOUS ARTICLES. ARK CURTAINS. TORAH COVERS. PORCHE-
SEN AND MANTLES. ALL OUR TALAISIM APPENDED BY KOSHER
ZTITZUS.

I leaned against Kipler's barbershop pole to rest a moment. Something was wrong with its mechanism and
the pole had been spinning two months continuously.
In the hollow base of the candystripe pole, Kipler kept
a paperbag full of clipped hair, into which he occasionally thrust the incriminating chits of his flourishing
numbers racket. At one time or another, everyone had
said to Kipler: "Quit messing up my hair with your il-
legal fortune." To which Kipler always replied: "I got

Pomade and Fitch for my lawyers, what's your hair got to worry about?"

In front of our building a sidewalk hole extended halfway into the gutter. A red lantern swung in the wind from an orange barricade. I had to pick my way round the muddle and, as I managed it, I remembered the desperation in Baron's voice when he spoke of the destruction of our city. "Every street is obsolete, we're being funneled and dug to clear a bit of leeway for too many relaxing bowels. Give us this day our daily purge."

Just behind our old-fashioned glass door, a stone step off the street, two Puerto Rican women were sitting on milkcases in the vestibule. They were old, beyond the furthest hangnail of age. Each wore a combat jacket (a gift of her G.I. grandson) under a dazzling white-knit shawl (a gift of her daughter-in-law). These two were always there to pass between. They laughed like children as you went by. They slapped at each other's hands. Sometimes one would work at a soft melody while the other grinned and nodded. Now, they sat facing each other, silent and free from silliness. In the cold each nuzzled a private whimsy, with the wordless affection the old have for themselves.

I said hello. They said nothing. Knowing they would not understand, I said: "Don't think about death so much. You see there are no alternatives. Don't think about it so much. Promise?"

"Goo nye," they said.

Going up the stairs, I rested on each landing. A draft hurried up behind me. Bibber's door was open an inch. On it he had tacked a yellowing pasteboard:

DON'T BE A DAY LATE, A DOLLAR SHORT—VOTE REPUBLICAN.

I pounded on his door.

"I'm reading Talmud—watch your step!"

"It's me—Barney Yago."

"If you're a holdup man, I'll bust my own head open. If you want to read the meter, I don't believe you, so you must be my father. I was raised an orphan. If you're the police, it wasn't Bibber threw out the bag of garbage from the window—it was Leibush on top of me. If you're Mrs. Cahoon, I'm in no mood for your songs. If you're a friend, you're here emptyhanded. If you're a girl, you'll laugh at my holiness. Call me Rambam— not the one who married at twelve. With Saladin I played pisha-paysha. What's wrong? —*n'shuma kron-keit?* My brother died with a pocket full of diamonds. That's me, *resh mem bes mem.* I hate the rubberband rings on your thighs. If you're Cahoon, drop dead. If you're a cat, I'll wash you in kerosene. I'm spotless. Meeow meeow meeow—I'm a fourlegged torch."

In the naked light he was at his kitchen table. Above him, the bulb aimed its archaic tit at a birthmark on his forearm. And above the bulb a score of rent receipts were taped to the single wire for ready evidence. Old before his time, yet quite old, very thin, with a caved-in chest, his head too small for the size of his ears, with a purple boil on his nose and his lips cracked, he wore his new black *shtrom'l,* its fur wheel fresh and glossy, his tiny gold collarbutton in a collarless shirt, his *tallis-kot'n,* his patriarch's smell, his beard. A hearing-aid case hung from his coat lapel by a paper clip. He called it "my Willkie button." On either ear the helix was as red as a winesap. On the table between his arms were copies of Mishna and Tosvoth, of Rashi, the Targum of Onkelos, of Moreh Nebuhim.

He did not look up as I entered. On a page of Mishna

sat a saucer of Indian nuts. He spat shells onto the books, then snapped them away with a finger.

"It's me," I said.

He looked up.

"Oho—the storyteller!"

He spit another nutshell. "You don't know enough to slap at a doorjamb? What's the *mezuzah,* a blindspot with you? Come in if you're in." He pushed the saucer of nuts toward me. Then he returned to his books. For what was I but a wooden leg bumping through Goydom?

He ignored me. His lips moved, a monotonic buzz alive in his mouth. (I'm removed from you wholly through an act of self. I'm unfettered.) Suddenly, with a mystical, a dark and esoteric tilt to his head, he closed his eyes and said: *"Genug."* (Now you know the value of Talmud. Each man is unique.)

I stood at his table waiting for an invitation to sit. He smiled at me. (I am an affirmation, Mr. Yago with no identity; I take to myself with wonder and delight.)

"Well, storyteller, what's new with the neighborhood Hitlers?"

"Bibber—I saw your cousin Baron on Friday. But first of all, you promised me you're getting rid of all these posters on the wall. This kitchen looks like a campaign headquarters for the Republican party."

"Hanh?" He put a finger into his ear and gave it a therapeutic shake. "Ah, these batteries. To me your voice sounds like a new shoe. I've been getting such strange noises, my son. For two weeks. Like the pipes knocking. Like the I.R.T. pulling into a station. Excuse the finger in the dike, Madam, the floodgates is busted."

I yelled my question at him. The smile left his face. His scorn was unconcealed.

Bibber was bent and bald. He hardly removed his
shtrom'l and most always slept sitting up. He was
genuinely deaf in his right ear. His Willkie button was
not worth the electric it ran on, so he had often com-
plained. I had long ago learned that his left ear was an
instrument for defense, clicking on and off as the occasion required. A little bitterness, a little criticism—it
clicked off, dead as paste.

"Hanh?" he said again, placing himself beyond hurt,
beyond reproach. (One thing, Mr. Storyteller Yago, one
of the injured, or insulted, I'll nevermore become.)

"Hanh? Hanh?"

He knew that I saw through him, but he knew, in
addition, that, to maintain our friendship I must respect
his rights of expression. He would carry on this harmless fiction of his deafness until his lids would be stepped
on by pennies over the sightless eyes.

"I'll tell you why Republican," he suddenly said. "You
are and you always will be and were never different, an
American. A city person. A New Yorker. You live in
America."

"Always and forever."

"I live in Babylon."

"Ah—why, you old thief! —You connive to the favor
of the host! Bibber, the Democrats are in power!"

"Some storyteller. The Democrats are in office; who
said they're in power?"

"And the Republicans represent your very special interests?"

"You're putting words in your own mouth. Listen,
Wednesday night I'm going to the baths; would you
like to come? On me!"

"I'll let you know."

"All right, I'll talk to Leibush."

Then, surprisingly, he removed his *shtrom'l*. "You're trying to put a brass ring through my nose, you *shtik luksh!*"

He rose, walked to his kitchentub storagebin. I followed him to lend a hand. During my visits this activity was ritual. Fishspines swam through his tub among books with no bindings. Moldy breadheels marched over tangerine pits and skullcaps. An onionshale blizzard had buried more books with places marked by cucumber rinds. This was his need, the skin of his skin, the blood of his blood.

With his back to me now, he undertook the salvation of his pride, his dignity and virtue, by soothing the chaos in his kitchentub bin. To Bibber I had sprung from an entire generation whose central passion had been to dance into the Gentile guard. But I was not an abstraction beyond his moral justice; I was not an opinion. I was a neighbor for whom he could not deny affection. I must have been the worst Jew of all, a real live *gilgul*. Like the boil on his nose which never healed, I forever oozed my jewness. I was impaled on the fact of that jewness—the bait, the fish, the hook, all at once. I was an *umglick* with my leg off. But that was the least of my misfortunes.

The faucet whistled as he wet a rag. He gave me a few things to hold, then dropped on his knees and began scrubbing at baseboards. On all fours, breathing heavily, he said: "So you went to see Baron?"

"Friday morning."

"And?"

"Why did you send me to him?"

"Hah! I wanted to show you what kind of cousin I've got!"

"That joke has a green beard on it, Bibber."

"And did he give you a ride in that famous flying machine of his?"

"He did. But I want to know why you sent me to him. You knew from the outset it would be ridiculous."

"Don't tell me what I knew from the outset. Outset. All of a sudden we're using words. I knew Baron would be ridiculous, not *it*. And being ridiculous, it's not so ridiculous that he would give you a job. I take it he didn't. Which is also ridiculous. I'm sorry. I wrote him a letter."

"He tore it up under my nose."

"That's the letter's fault?"

To the last detail, I described my meeting with Baron. Still on his knees, Bibber straightened, arched his back.

"You mean he really showed you his doors?"

"Yes."

"A triumph. You should be honored. A person must have a special *smell* about him before Baron introduces him to his doors. Do you know what his trouble is? *Ehr's in zein tatte gerut'n.* The man is without a conscience. Oh, I knew his father very well. A different man altogether from his brother—who was *my* father. Everything in Baron is manufactured, so very complicated. Why blame me, Barney? On the basis of these complications which I know so well I naturally decided that he'd fit you in somewhere, merely as a reaction to *me*. Catch on? Don't be discouraged. There are plenty of jobs. Aaaf! There are men worse off than Baron. Take Cahoon."

He smiled and said not another word. He walked on his knees to the sink. He wrung the wet rag dry. Then he turned to me and with a deliberate show passed his tongue between his teeth. At the mention of Cahoon we had both struck our familiar silence. In this way the janitor became the subject of an old understanding between us.

(Poor Cahoon! Out of touch with God, who, after all, knew the man's heart, and out of touch with Satan, because of the bitter baptismal wound. Ah, the Church! The Church! The irritable picklepuss janitor! Unlucky enough to be born what he'll die. To shovel his life away into that furnace, way down under six disgraceful floors, fallen way down yet not low enough, and we, his *yidls*, his *yidls*, piled up high on top of him.)

Bibber rose up in a creak and threw his muddy rag into the sink. Taking his books out of my hands, he flung them as before into his kitchentub bin. He was wrung like his rag by his own emotion, but not quite enough to dispel his big, cunning smile. (I'm sick and tired of explaining myself. Which is to explain truth.)

"My cousin Baron is worse off than a Roumanian who dreams of lying in a tomb built of cold *momme-liggeh*."

"*Momme* what*geh?*"

"Yellow cornmeal. Sometimes eaten with cheese. Or maybe he's even worse off than that Sicilian *knyocker* of yours down in Two G. *That* one dreams of a whorehouse in heaven."

"Quastafesti loves to clown."

"You're angry with me?"

"No. I don't know, Bibber. Yes. Yes and no. Yes, I am. I mean that whole episode with Baron—I appreciate your efforts, the letter and so forth, but I've got the feeling that you didn't half believe in it yourself."

"You talk so childish."

He waved his hand at me and put a match under the teakettle.

"Barney, my son—why are we at each other's throats?"
He dredged his teabag through a cup of hot water. "Life
is too old, Barney."

He bit into a slice of bread as thick as a book. Then,
with his eyes closed, he sipped at his tea.

"Whawh—hot!" (I am gutted and skinned and
wrung milkless with life. Me, Bibber. Me, the most brilliant linguist in all of Lodz. When I was a boy I held all
Europe to my ear like a warm shell. Now I'm here—
America is the front page of a newspaper—an unscalable
wall.)

"Aaf, Barney, . . . believe me, please believe me, they
should have left me in Auschwitz. They should have,
they should have. I know what I'm talking about. I was
happy to wander through my valley of dry bones. All I
wanted was to find a single charred splinter that was
part of my wife. Why didn't they leave me alone? . . .
I was on the right track. And the smoke that my four
children went up in I smelled at dawn. Do you know it
made me a new man? Does it give you anything to
think abut?"

When he stopped talking to finish his tea, he proceeded, with wet cheeks, to set in motion round me a
studied routine of preparation, full of kindly solicitations to himself, setting his kitchen in subjective order,
switching off the naked overhead, adjusting a lamp,
kicking off his shoes, polishing his glasses, putting his
saucer of Indian nuts on the crippled arm of an over-
stuffed chair. Each step was categorical and precise, full
of mystery, equal in weight and gravity to the one before
and the one following, each consuming an identical
span in the measured chain, and my presence did not
disturb him. Kingly and oracular he walked through
his ceremony, a little mean, a little joyous. Then, he sat

down. I stood up. (I hadn't been there at all. Did not, in fact, exist.) He slapped and pounded at a newspaper. He began to read with his mouth. His head rolled. His eyes closed. His head bobbed and tossed and sprang up rigid. He forced his eyes to open. He put two fingers on his Willkie button.

"Bibber?"

He was motionless, his eyes so wide now he was quite frightening.

His fingers relaxed, his hands fell open onto his lap, the paper onto his stomach. Over the floors his snores rattled along.

I came out of Bibber's and met the sound of strangulation. Starting up the stairs, I heard it again. When I reached the fifth floor I saw Zena Cudcik there. Death, her companion for so many years, had suddenly assumed a punitive role and tacked her thumbs to an apartment door.

"What's the matter? . . . Mrs. Cudcik? . . . How'd you get up here? . . ."

In her nightgown and barefooted she had propped herself in a stiff, semi-upright position, her palms flat against a door, her body a good step away, a brittle hypotenuse opposite the threshold.

"Mrs. Cudcik!"

She broke in two. Her palms slid down the door but never left it. Some mysterious recoil shot her straight as a stick. Reaching her maxiumum thrust, her eyes fixed square on the apartment number—4E. Out of her throat came a child's melody of whups and whees.

"Hold on!—I'll get Cahoon—"

Mortars went off behind a ridge: four doors shutting.

Then a mortar went off right behind me, trailed by a slap of slippers. It was Bailey, the sodaman.

"What's going on? Hey—look at her nightgown!"

He retreated to his apartment door. "What's going on?"

"Get Cahoon, Mr. Bailey!"

Barewaisted, his hairy biceps were full of freckles and babypowder.

"Get Cahoon, for God's sakes!"

The injunction chilled him. He ran into his apartment and came out again struggling into a sweater, his head and arms making a simultaneous appearance through it.

"Look at her nightgown!" he said and flew down the stairs. "Is she gagging?" his voice called up, passing him on the way.

Made of some lavish white material, her nightgown billowed round her in the lash and gale of her attack.

"Do you want some water, Mrs. Cudcik?"

She managed to turn her head and look into my eyes. Water to a drowning woman! My question struck her forcibly. She raised one hand away from her door-prop, indicating that my own affliction was surely equal to hers.

"Aaaaah—Barney—omblints—omblints, Barney—"

"Hold on, Mrs. Cudcik, we're getting one."

"Good Jesus, is she kiddin' herself out of a shroud?" Cahoon said, rushing up the stairs. Bailey was immediately behind him and little Jenny immediately behind Bailey.

"I think it's an asthma attack, Mr. Cahoon. Did somebody call an ambulance?"

"I did," Bailey said.

"But look at the nightgown! What do we do, just stand around?"

"Blow into her mouth like they do a baby," Bailey said.

"You're an idiot, Mr. Bailey," Cahoon said. "What do we do, Mr. Yago?"

"I don't know."

Little Jenny, hoping to pluck the matter away from us ran into Bailey's apartment and reappeared with a chair and a glass of milk. The old lady sat down and knocked the glass out of the little girl's hand. Milk and glass crashed down the steps.

"Jesus—get a pan and broom, Jenny—there'll be people walkin' barefoot," Cahoon said.

Great rivers of color, red and green and gold, raced over Zena's nightgown, cascading off her shoulders to swirl round her waist. Like a snarl of wild grapes, a variety of heavy beads hung from her neck. Tangled up in the glass vine was a brass crucifix. Little Jenny, back with pan and broom, began to brush up the bits of glass. Under her arm were rags to sop the milk.

Zena hawked and sputed. The crucifix leaped in the glass vine. The old lady trembled metallically.

"How'd she get up here? Did she come down Tenth Street dressed like that?" Cahoon said. "In this freezin' cold?"

Little Jenny ran down the stairs with pan, broom, and sopping rags held stiffly. "See if your mother's comin'," Cahoon called after her.

He said to me: "She's got no business bein' dressed in that outfit. Good Jesus. You couldn't near lay her away in an ordinary coffin dressed like that. She'll overflow and run out. Excuse me—I mean, should the old lady pass on."

Zena shot up from her chair. She twisted away, she shook, she seemed to reel under a violent blow. Even in

our light her skin was purified into a thin cerulean blue.
As if to damn her dark hysteria with a mark of frivolity,
she threw her arms heavenward, striking a pose. She
sprang forward, hooping me round the neck. Bands of
steel. I hooped her back. Her brass crucifix lodged between her cheek and my neck. It cut my skin. I bled.
Neither Cahoon nor Bailey came forward to help. The
old lady had lurched me into a jig. Spots of my blood
were on her arms. Out of her throat came those unholy
lung squalls. Our three usable legs surpassed any four
—though my willow limb dragged unmercifully. She
clung to me for a time beyond belief. Had I not gripped
her with all my strength we would have tumbled from
her catwalk. Her beads pecked at my face like bugs.
And then, quite suddenly, her head spilled limply and
bumped my shoulder ever so softly. There, in front of
4E, the old woman shivered and pitched. She fell oystery
and slick out of her ancient shell. She died in my tightest
hug.

Up the crepuscular, stifflegged stairs, over the glutted
landings, squeezing two-by-two through the sweating
halls wide enough for one, past the mortarshot thump
of door after door, came our neighbors soft and seeking,
some to help and some to hinder, some to cry, some to
giggle, some to lord it and some to squint, some to make
alliances, some to break them, some to be sick and some
indifferent, some with children in their arms, one with
a shiny eggplant. Some came for a moment's reflection,
some to invent a profound loss, some to rub shoulders
with the inevitable police, some to enjoy the doctor's
work. One with a paintbrush, one with a can of soup,
and a boy was there with his tiny toy sled. Some came

to calculate, some to transcend, some to be simply harassed.

Quastafesti, the dollmaker, had once said: "Our city is full of hidden death which forces a stand on the issue of living."

When Esther Cahoon arrived, she was holding a bingo card.

"I was over at St. Emeric's. I had a feeling—oh, Mama! Mama!"

Our neighbors were in a crush around Zena's body. It lay sadly on the floor, as if her death had been her compliance to an order of eviction, whereupon some kind neighbor had set her on the curb, in the dead of night, to await the City Marshal's truck. Within our narrow halls Esther could not sift through the crush. Bailey, the sodaman, pushed her hard enough to send her through, and it stirred us all into a prodigious ballet.

A Bellevue interne was kneeling at the body. She had just put a final needle into the old lady. She wiped the needle with a cotton ball. A big woman whose bosom drove apart her starchycrisp lapels like tent flaps, the interne was an exquisitely skinned Negro, mature, played-out, though fastidious in handling her medical kit.

"I had a feeling!" Esther said again through tiny sobs. "Poor mama!"

Mrs. Tartock, from 4F down the hall, put a green cloth coat with a muskrat collar over Zena Cudcik.

The interne rose up on her mighty thighs. Her starchycrisp sleeves were specked with iodine.

"I had a feeling," Esther said again. Cahoon, comfortable in deception, put a comforting arm round his wife.

The interne borrowed a flashlight from a nearby cop and lit up her little blue pad, into which she began to write.

"D.O.A." she said.

"Precinct has a call in for the Examiner's office," the cop said.

The interne smiled, and I thought I even heard a soft chuckle, as if our mismanagement of the event amused her. "Who's next of kin?" she asked. "Is there a next of kin?" she asked, without raising her eyes from her little blue pad. She simply refused to look at anybody, and her question was stamped in formality.

"I'm her daughter."

The interne's smile was fixed. She kept on writing, and smiling, while Esther talked.

"What about the remains, Doc?" the cop asked.

"A dock is where a ship ties up, Officer." She returned his flashlight. "The remains remain until the Examiner gets here."

The cop made a brave effort to clear the hall. The steamy yellow air laid a harsh, yet sickly, discoloration on his face. Several Puerto Ricans navigated their children down the stairs with a clear exultancy, while the unending tattoo of their words, as headless and hard as finishing nails, reconstructed Zena's death.

Esther Cahoon let out a heartsick cry.

The interne chinked with her finger at the cop's badge. "Mister, do you have any idea what a pit our city really is?"

She packed her bag and said goodbye. The cop had some success in clearing the hall. My wet stump sock had begun to chafe. Our light was now a glutinous gray char. Zena's body lay where it fell to await the medical examiner. Over Mrs. Tartock's green cloth coat someone had put a patchwork featherquilt. The cop's flashlight threw laboring shadows on the walls. Cahoon kept his arm round Esther, who had buried her face in his neck, and she softly wept, with her own arm round little Jenny, who had buried her head inside Esther's open coat. Except for the scroop of a bad door, the crack of a knuckle, the blat of a voice, the crack of a nutshell underfoot, nothing of a public nature remained at hand.

Esther Cahoon turned to those of us who were left. "Oh, I'm sorry it had to happen like this—I mean, I don't know why she came up here—I mean, it isn't even my floor—I mean, it was bingonight—will they leave her there for long?"

"Now, dear—shhhh—she can't be disturbed until the coroner comes," Cahoon said.

"God, the pickle I'm in."

"Dear, she must have had something left at the end. I mean, it took a fine nobility to come down Tenth Street in that highly personal nightgown knowin' that time was runnin' out."

"Oh God the pickle I'm in—"

"Shhhhh, dear—shhhh—"

"I'm lost."

"She was very old, my sweet. She's been awful sick for a long time. You knew that."

"Mama! —Mama, I'm lost—"

"Now don't go on like that. There's little Jenny. There's your husband, your home."

"My mother is dead!"

Shivering in a sad little cotton coat, a cold red shawl wound thickly round her neck, Mildred Osot, from 4G on the court, stepped behind Cahoon. Without a word of apology she knocked on his shoulderblade. With a damp ball of cloth she pecked at her nose.

"Mister—old womans too long lay on floor—"

Cahoon turned to her. "Oh, Mrs. Osot—"

"Too long lay on floor." She admonished Cahoon with rapid little sounds of tongue on palate.

"I sugra burn."

"There's no need for that," Cahoon said.

"I sugra burn."

"Mrs. Osot—they'll be takin' her out in a minute."

Mrs. Osot had a girlish, melancholy way. She sobbed and shook her head, and her large amethyst earrings pendulated wildly. Through the wreck of an English noun, through a snip and driblet of German and Polish, she dramatized Zena's body, lying there so powerfully unboxed, a desperate fizzing in her nose. She kept slapping her palms together and sobbing, peevishly yet mystically embittered by our New York atmosphere, by the filth we were forced to suck into ourselves—a filth which had surely killed Zena Cudcik, which was killing her husband, which would ultimately kill us all. A big city, this is the evil.

As she spoke in her gruel of stepmother tongues, as Cahoon tried to shush her, she pointed her nose straight up. Like a tiny motor it puttputted and sniffed, as she poked her finger through the air, to stab every little flake of filth we were soon to paste on our lungs. (Rivers and rainbows of phlegm bubble along our curbs. Lung and nostril, that's what we are in our New York America—a mass asphyxia.)

"Konchur!" Mrs. Osot cried out.

"Shhh—it's not cancer, Mrs. Osot. Now, it isn't cancer which killed Mrs. Cudcik," Cahoon said.

"I sugra burn! —konchur—hull vurlt full ir'rotten

konchur! Mek childs dumb cracy steal evertink stupid!
—husbont Osot got konchur vurk down bank he dead
soon wit luffly gun—on job konchur kill Osot soon—"

"I'm sorry about Mr. Osot, my dear—but now is not
the time."

"Hull vurlt got konchur, mister—mek you stupid
cracy steal pockabook poor womans hurt evertink—I
sugra burn!"

"You sugra burn in your own damn apartment! Now
there's no need for your nonsense, Mrs. Osot. —You
hear me?"

Cahoon turned to me and said: "In such a state, what
can you drum up for people? Lord, I'm glad I sent
Esther and the kid downstairs."

"You can't deceive Mrs. Osot, Mr. Cahoon. I mean,
about her husband. Any advice merely fattens the ad-
visor."

"Did y'know thay've put a sheepshank on the poor
man's lower bowel? He's got a little gauze bag hangin'
on his belly."

"Then you can imagine what it must be doing to
her."

"Ah, the man is only a bankguard, but to this one
he's a shining admiral. I tell you, son . . . she's been
taken in by his sidearm holster. Oh, she adores the man,
adores him!"

Turning back to Mrs. Osot, who had been quietly
studying Zena's body, Cahoon quickly became a wag-
ging finger of authority.

She slapped Cahoon hard across the face and ran
into her apartment.

"Good Jesus! The goddam woman is unhinged! Did
you see that look of spite on her face, Mr. Yago?"

Mrs. Osot was back again, carrying a bowl full of

brown sugar, over which she had poured alcohol, to which she had put a match. "I sugra burn!" she yelled.

She held the ball of blue flame aloft, a melting mass of mythic grandeur, and the flame whooshed and died while the mass smoked. The bowl simply grew too hot. She dropped it crashing at Zena's body. Her face lit up with a marveling smile. Her graying hair was peppered with singe. She hopped and stomped over the hot rubble; the tip of Mrs. Tartock's muskrat collar had begun to smolder. Cahoon kicked at it. In his rage he had knocked off his eyepatch; it now hung by its string absurdly from an ear, exposing his dark and fleshred eyecave. The sodaman Bailey, brought again into the hall by this new commotion, pinned Mrs. Osot's arms from behind and dragged her, laughing and crying, into her apartment. "I sugra burn! Ir'rotten konchur evertink!"

"To hell with you!" Cahoon yelled. "To hell with all you disgusting lot!"

The policeman who had been posted at the remains to await the medical examiner rushed out of Mrs. Tartock's apartment, where he had gone to write his report. He chased the remaining few of us from the scene. As I walked away, I noticed the sour look which had taken hold of the policeman's face. He was now left alone with an old lady's corpse, there in our hall's twilight.

I hurried out of the building. I'd felt lost among the lost and dead in our hall. I walked all the way to Union Square.

There, a great stone horse canters beautifully toward Broadway. From under its rump I watched a bright new flake being mocked by a driving gust. The flake was swung round and round, swung under a bench and over a tree. Ultimately, it flew onto the equestrian's heroic eyelid. But the flake had already multiplied to seed the streets of the city, had danced and ridden the wind until, with unsurprising suddenness, the night was alive with snow. Parked cars were bisons, ghostly and white, trooping headless in a standstill file.

When I returned, defeated by the snow, they had already carried Zena Cudcik away.

And, finally, after the long, long day, I climbed the stairs, when things were quiet. And I heard my phantoms come to call.

They slid in their pink skins off the mounting stair of silence, red teeth clacking, whirling a tortuous dance. Five phantoms in all. Big toe to little toe. In 2H a baby cried; my phantoms lurched into their dance of the toes. They wiggled, they stomped, they screeched. My pink devils. Five snakes in a boot. They spat. They bit. They gnawed at the flesh. Born in innocence, they cartwheeled, jackknifed; they catsprung and highjumped. They chinned on the bars of my stump's living nerves. In 3F a toilet gurgled; my phantoms turned somersault. All the hideous ghosts of my whilom toes which lay buried under the black heart of a German forest. But they were here with me now in our hall's bastard light; here, not on my stump's mouth, but there, rightly, in the place they belonged, each toe alone, and all five assembled, twitching, peeling, bending, reeling and flexing, affixed to a plane through space where my foot might have been, on the rim of a cylinder of space where my leg might have been. The stump yawped; laden with cargo, it reached, then retched, and it pushed over my mind's precipice, trying to fill up this cylinder

of space, to implant its root in the plane of the space of
my foot, to fill up that nothingness across which my
toes were truly stretched.

Later that morning, the florist's boy tacked a blackribboned wreath on the wrong door. The error was discovered by Mrs. Osot, our building's earliest riser. The
wrong door belonged to the Tartocks, who occupied
the two rooms squeezed between Bibber's and mine.

Mrs. Osot, who was on her way down to Tepp, the
fruit man, for breakfast oranges, bled superstition from
every pore. To put a glass of water to your lips was to
surrender yourself to a witch's brew. With wood and
with mustard, with curries and herbs and quartered
peppercorns, Mrs. Osot sought our salvation. More and
more she relied on her oaths and curses and, at the smallest sign of sickness or death, she would dash into our
halls with her purifying bowl of sugar. As her husband
grew worse in his cancer, her crusade against our city's
filth became intense and bitter.

Yet whirling through her energies was a certain elegance, a certain femininity. Once, by chance, she and I,
in the shadows of our courtyard, witnessed the birth of
a baby to a Puerto Rican woman whose husband had
deserted her, and whose fear had, at the last moment,
driven her out of her rooms. The poor woman could
not find for herself an excess of debasement, so she had
picked out this littered alcove in the court, near the cellar door, foul, and putrid, and crawling with tiny white
maggots. Mrs. Osot and I, coming into the hall at the
same time, heard the woman's cries. We could not coax
her back indoors. Mrs. Osot ran to phone for an ambulance and returned with a clean blanket. She persuaded
the woman to at least move to a cleaner spot. As she

spread the blanket I noticed she had, with a determined prissiness, become another woman. She was now dressed in a dry, somber, severely cut gray suit, and a simple white blouse. At her throat was a demure puff of white collar. She handed me her neat little hat with a blue ribbon, and a small black boxlike purse. It was as if she had flung herself back on some stern tribal discipline to pluck the poor woman out of her terror. The ambulance arrived as Mrs. Osot was wrapping the baby in two of Mr. Osot's fresh white shirts. . . .

The commotion brought me out into the hall. Mrs. Tartock, defeated by Mrs. Osot's hysteria, had, just as I came out, run back into her apartment. Mr. Tartock, who took his wife's place, seemed to have a calming effect on Mrs. Osot.

"The boy made a mistake, Mrs. Osot. Here, look, look at the card. Don't you see? Zena Cudcik, beloved mother of Esther Cahoon. You see? Ah, she can't *read!* Look, lady—in my rooms nobody will be receiving one of these for a long, long time. I guarantee you that. It doesn't mean a thing. It's just a common, everyday mistake."

He pulled the wreath down and held it behind him. With his other hand he patted Mrs. Osot's shoulder. "Go about your business, Mrs. Osot—there's nothing to it."

Tartock, a nightworker, was doing his best to deal in moderation with his neighbor. He had always considered her a ridiculous woman whose sole function in life was to prevent his sleeping. Persuaded, Mrs. Osot left, hurrying down the stairs with her noisy shopping bag.

"If it's not one thing, it's another," he said to me, in a surprising lapse, for he always kept to himself. "Four mornings in a row she's been out here banging on my door. For this, for that, for the other. My wife is afraid of her own shadow, so to her a knock on the door is something fierce. You can imagine. Out of bed I have to tumble to face this Mrs. Osot. My luck."

Tartock had the nightworker's pallor. He was a track-walker for the B.M.T. A small, shy man, he suffered from anemia. He was always short of breath, which gave him the appearance of rushing through life, when the opposite was true. His eyes bulged, sitting inside the red rings of a chronic conjunctivitis. He had a long head. His face was soft and his skin had a weak shine.

"Why do people go on living here? I was married in these rooms, thirty-three years ago. But you should have seen this building then. The whole neighborhood was proud of it; people were dying to get in here. Can you beat it? Ah, I'll die here—and before my time, believe me."

As I said, Tartock was, by nature, a withdrawn man. Most people considered him a miser. It was common knowledge that he did not believe in banks, bonds, real estate, insurance. Some said that his hoard in cash was terrific, even greater than the barber Kipler's. Quastafesti had called Tartock an authentic miser, the last of a true breed, who put Pere Grandet to shame. I'd never seen a new stick of furniture, a new pot, or dish cross over his threshold. His quiet ways naturally induced mistrust. Mrs. Osot was the only soul who had ever felt free enough to knock at the Tartock door.

Mrs. Tartock kept her husband's hours. She had the same red eyes, the same weak shine on her skin. She also had a mania for cleanliness. Every evening at six, when her husband woke up, she sleepily scrubbed down the small patch of hall directly at her door. She constantly washed and waxed her doorjambs, and the door itself. Her door belonged in another place.

When you passed her on the stairs she looked the other way. I had heard that Mrs. Tartock was a Christian Scientist—which thoroughly embarrassed her husband —though one day, through her door which was accidentally ajar, I had seen her moving about in the bonnet and cape of the Salvation Army.

Before I knew it, right there in the hall, Tartock had so many things to say I could hardly keep up with him. He was a newspaper student; he read all of them through, every day. His brain was a conglomerate pudding of statistic and opinion. He was delighted with my attention and forgot about his put-upon sleep. Then, in the midst of a cynical narration on the meaning of earning a living underground, he said: "To hell with it. What do you know about it? To hell with it. We're in a depression. You think no? How much do they expect us to take? Mark my word. Remember the last depression? Were you even alive? It swung by me in a bucket, you know that? That's right, the whole depression, right in this tin bucket."

"I don't get you, Mr. Tartock."

"There was a man's head in the bucket. A big depositor in the banks. Just a plain tin bucket that swung under my nose. He jumped under a train and I was standing there when they brought his head down from the El tracks. I can still see the eyes, and the slick pad of hair. God, those eyes!—tiny and dry and just as blue and stupid as an eel's."

"He didn't have to do that," I said.

"Do what?"

"Jump under the train. He might have had a little patience. Most people got back a good percent of their money."

"For God's *sake!* Thirty billion dollars in capital values just swept away—*poosh!*"

He turned away from me. I had injured him. Then, he held up the blackribboned wreath and shook it at me. "This is the work of your friend Quastafesti. Oh, don't tell *me!* Him and his practical jokes—it was him told that flower boy to tack it on my door! I won't dignify it by bringing it up again. The lousy bomb-thrower!"

His intention was to slam the door in my face. But his wife had locked him out. When she finally let him in I saw once again her strange, red-eyed face tied round with the crisp little bonnet of the Salvation Army.

I brought Tartock's accusation to Quastafesti. "Of course," he said, "why not? Why shouldn't he blame me? The man is a poor little fish and I'm his gaff. We both moved into this building years ago on the same day—there was something in that coincidence which drove him mad. I can't fathom any other reason for the way he's been after me all these years."

"But what's he really got against you, Vincent?"

"Who knows? Of course, you don't believe me. I'm telling you every man is a receptacle for another's spleen. I'm Tartock's. Why do you think he devours all those newspapers every day? They simply provide him with raw material—he can pin all the earth's grief on *me!* No, no—it's the truth. What's that Yiddish word that Bibber always uses?—to describe the common every-day wretchedness that boils under the skin?—that thread of rancor that spools out unbroken to the grave?"

"Grizhe?"

"Ah—I *grizhe* Tartock. D'you get me? It gives a unity
to his life. Supposing tomorrow he reads in his New
York *Times* that a blight of Newcastle threatens the
survival of all producing hens in the New York, New
Jersey, and Connecticut areas. My son, you can bet on it
that Tartock in his giant's metality will lay the original
source of the whole poultry infection on me! Why?
How? Who knows? Lay it to life. To the coincidence
that I'm alive on the same planet contemporaneously
with Mr. Andrew Tartock, trackwalker par excellence,
B.M.T. division. Ahh—for the love of Jesus, let's cut it
out—it depresses me!"

He was at his butcher's block, which he had con-
verted into a workbench. Bramovitch, on Avenue C,
had given him the block in exchange for several dolls
in Regency costume.

He was an expert dollmaker of the stuffed variety,
and his shop was the little shackly store at the front of
our building. He lived upstairs in 2G, with an eighty-
year-old father, and Gilda, his twin sister, who was in-
sane.

Vincent was long, straight, and smooth, with a prominent Adam's apple. The saddest eyes I had ever seen sat
moist and incredulous in an otherwise tranquil face.
And in his hands a book, always a book; the mark of
the pedagogue.

In our talks I'd often detect a ferocity which was hard
to understand. "I cannot believe in your dedication,"
he had said, "until it arrives at the tailend of your experience. Don't give me this business about losing your
leg—I've got too many years on you. That is an experience of the narrowest kind. What about the practice of
living? You're making yourself inept. You are going

to stumble to your grave through your own ineptitude."

"I have no other choice, Vincent."

"Isolation is the path of the coward."

I was always forced to ask him why, in his own case, he had closeted himself in that dingy little shop to spin his life out pounding sawdust into rag dolls. "Why, why—I hate the specialization of labor, that's why." And he would stalk away from me, angered. It was with Vincent I learned how hard most true friendships are.

He worked at night. "Night is essential to the outcast," he would say. "Jack London knew what he was talking about."

Frequently we walked to the yellow cafeteria on Irving Place and talked the night away over a parade of coffee cups.

"I used to come to this place when I was younger," Vincent once said. "Some of the finest minds in the country sat around this very table. What's happened to them? They're all dead of food poisoning."

AN EARLIER TUESDAY

ᕼᕉ ON ONE OF THOSE CAFETERIA NIGHTS VINCENT WAS injured. Occupying two floors above the place were the meeting rooms of the Sons of the Knights of Virbius. Gerald Palamino, a boyhood friend of Vincent and a current Chancellor, had invited him to enjoy the Chapter's well-stocked library. Vincent and I exploited this privilege and went there.

The main hall was a huge, berugged oval. From its

hub rose a round cleverly constructed stage, and at two
points in the hall's circumference wide stairs led to a
girdling balcony, and further to a variety of small ad-
ministrative rooms. National, State, and Local Chapter
flags were draped throughout the hall. A bar, lit up by
cylinders of rose fluorescence, swerved round a segment
of wall. The silken perimeter was jeweled by giant, cali-
brated eyes swollen with copper veins and sprouting
English darts.

That Tuesday night we hadn't expected the music,
or the dancing, or the carnival atmosphere. "It's a social,"
Vincent said. "They must be having an installation. God,
look at their women!"

Very soon, Vincent and I were dancing. My dancing
was absurd, grotesque; risking it, a woman displayed
her sweetness in rising above my oneleggedness.

A whitehaired lady tossed a corsage off the balcony.
The trio onstage erupted. Virbius danced and writhed,
hungry for extremes. A short, feverish man kept pumping my hand and congratulating himself on the dazzling affair (they had bagged several prominent young
men, among whom were people high in government
and business, a young jurist, a half-dozen or so profes-
sionals, and a flourishing young physicist, said to be the
pride of Park Slope). With gelatinous jowls and chubby
fingers this man, who would not let go of my hand,
counted off a catalog of names, and suddenly tried to
engage me in an exchange of smut. He was expert at
forcing me into those small puerile obscenities of the
male brotherhood. Palamino, Vincent's friend, who had
joined us at the bar, tried to outdo him. Palamino was
the youngest Congressman in the history of our District,
a brilliant lawyer and a renowned fighter for slum clear-
ance. He was a darkeyed, blonde, honeyvoiced man

whose soft brown mustache moved like seaweed in a
pool over his limp mouth. His humor depended on
mangled bodies and the perpetual confusion of genitalia
between animals and humans.

I was sitting at the bar facing him. I jammed two
fingers to the knuckles into the kneejoint slot in my
willow limb. It drove the pantleg in deep beneath the
patella. I had expected the sight to lodge in his throat
like a ball of hair. But he stood before me laughing,
laughing hyenically, as if my gesture had been a superb
punctuation upon his jokes.

Later, about the incident, Vincent said, "One man's
contentment is another's headache. That's life."

We were standing in the library just off the swerving
tier. We were able to hear the riot of cheering for the
entertainment onstage.

Suddenly, from the big hall, came a choral chant,
foreign to the patter of the entertainer. It rose faintly at
first, in a sustained sibilance, as though the chorus had
tried whistling before any commitment of voice. The
chant grew thicker, and louder. It was plain that some
mischief was taking hold. It rolled into the library in
waves, a kaleidoscope of sounds, gushing toward us
from the tier, from the paneled ceiling above, from the
walls of books, from the big hall itself, from the street
below, a roiling cacophony in mock and genuine dia-
lect—Spanish, Yiddish, Polish, Norwegian, Italian.

The lights went out.

"Good God!" Vincent yelled. "What's going on?"

The lights came on.

"Barney—you'd better get out of here!"

A bluish scarf of smoke curled under the lintel and
licked long against the ceiling and fanned out into a
cloud.

"It's a fire—Barney—this is no place for you! Get out of here!"

"Look out, Vincent!"

As he turned in the direction of the door, a tall, studious-looking boy was already in the library. He lashed out a length of wire cable, and its jagged tip caught Vincent under the eye. Then I heard a shattering of glass. The bar downstairs was toppled. This was an invasion of neighborhood hoodlums.

Vincent fell: the boy lashed his cable again, catching his neck. The boy let out a girlish shriek. I swung my cane, and kept swinging it round and round, through my fright, through my disbelief and rage, and it tore half the boy's ear off with a sickening crack. The cable flew out of his hands. His mouth fell slack, revealing a dental brace. He sagged to the floor, clutching his ear, and remained in a limp, kneeling position, his knees cushioned on Vincent's arm. The boy looked first at Vincent, then at me, senselessly, through a touching, doleful smile, his lips puckering and sucking fishlike at the air. I saw a dark fluid ooze from his mouth, and the blood flooding from his ear, the torn piece flapping free and weighty, like a hanging rind of fruit. Vincent, recovered, freed his arm and sprang up. His cheek had burst like a melon. "My God! It's a gang! My God, it must be that First Avenue gang!"

Now, for the first time, he seemed to notice the boy, who was still dumbly kneeling, his head fallen like a suppliant. "Who hit him? Did you hit him, Barney?"

"To hell with him. Let him alone. Let's get out of here —look at that smoke!"

I started to the door. "Let him alone, Vincent. Don't touch the bastard!"

"He's a child, Barney—he's hurt—"

"He's not a child. Don't touch him!"

Vincent ran to a water cooler. He tried to treat himself. There was a good deal of smoke now. The boy gagged and laughed. Revived by the smoke, he was once again malevolent. Unaffected by his mutilated ear, he remembered his cable lash, but could not find it. So he made for a cylinder ashtray. Vincent stepped in front of him to shield him against my threatening cane.

"If you hit this child again I swear I'll climb all over you!"

"Are you crazy?"

"Barney, there's a way to deal with this—"

"Let's get out of here!"

The boy then drove from behind the steelball tip of a spinner top. It went flush into Vincent's raw neck wound. An awful cry came out of him, and he brought his hands up to his face as I reached for him. The boy was already gone.

They were neighborhood boys who had swarmed through the rear windows and exits, descending from the roofs of adjoining buildings. They had shinnied and scaled stackpipes and fire escapes and rain gutters and inchwide ledges. They were driven by their own swift tyranny of movement, pursuing their youthful pleasure with an automatic unity of action, and for weapons they'd picked up everything along the way, for our city is an inexhaustible arsenal.

At the water cooler, which was on the outer tier, where I helped Vincent to come to, I saw some men deal with a heap of smoldering drapes, from which all the smoke had issued. The invaders outnumbered us. They were everywhere in the Virbius temple.

A squad of boys defended the toppled bar with swing-

ing pipes and barrel staves. At first, it seemed that a
single purpose drove them on. Yet it was plain that they
had no leaders; that each to the other, apart from a single
identity of dress and age, was a stranger. Each boy was
on the scene through a personal whim, through an accident of birth and residence, and his stake was purely in
arbitrary fires. Their action was empty, for it was borrowed from their victims. They had less concern for one
another than they had for us, their enemies. Even in
combat I had never seen truer anarchy. A vicious antag-
onism sprang up onstage, between two boys who'd been
clubbing at a common target side by side: the proud
young physicist of Park Slope. Badly bleeding, he escaped when his executioners became aware of each
other and turned on themselves. In the alcove behind the
bar, a girl, not more than fourteen, one of a dozen or
so accompanying the crusading horde like the concu-
bines of old, suddenly screamed for help: two of her
young crusaders had turned on her, ripped her clothes
away and now clawed at each other for rights of initial
possession, while the girl, half-naked, struggled on the
floor.

The big hall was filled with smoke—a strange, tinted
smoke which had poured from the balcony. Thin rivu-
lets of blood bubbled across the hard green carpet on the
main floor. In the angry red haze only eyes stood out
and red mouths and disembodied fists clutching makeshift weapons. Objects sailed through the air with a
weird merriment, while fragments of the wild frieze
hung in space, filled out from behind by spongy, amorphous shapes.

I would not leave my vantage point on the balcony,
but Vincent had rushed downstairs and was now on-

stage. He had put on a white and purple ceremonial robe. He was yelling. What, I could not make out. Then the stage was uprooted and he fell off.

Behind the upended bar a strange impasse had developed. The reflection of a line of children was drawn across the mirror. Several Virbius men gazed at it, then joined hands and moved toward it, as if to hold and pin the image in place, and make captives of the actual children behind them. All round them the shambles had intensified. From their young captives the Virbius men had taken back attitudes of hate and privilege. One man, the Sergeant-at-Arms, was taking stock; . . . he kept informing the captive line that the police were on their way. He yanked at his belt and pulled himself up with considerable relief. Through his cheek ran a slice, icy and taut, from his eye to his lower jaw. Then, seeing the young invaders stamped against the mirror, his outrage became uncontrollable. He wept. Several times his wife, a buxom woman now in shreds, tried to pull him away, but he knocked her aside. "Get me a glass of water," he yelled. "Get me a glass of water!"

Gerald Palamino hurried to him with a length of shackly chickenwire, which had been brought there by the invaders themselves. The Sergeant-at-Arms grabbed one end and together they stretched it across the image of the captive line. The children seemed to grow flatter, and flatter, and flatten into the surface of the mirror. They showed no fear. They were all in some way mutilated. Their eyes were sorrowful, yet waxy and dead. There was no means of securing the wire. These children with dead eyes, who were waiting for some action from their captors, did not revolt against their captivity. The wire cage plopped over. A tall, dark boy, whose nose was crushed, moved. And the movement leaped out not from the boy, but from the mirror itself. By now, they were well recessed into the glass surface, and became a part of it. They reflected, in their shimmering silvery skins, the violent motion opposite them. These images were less sharp than those leaping across areas which were still actual, unbroken mirror. It was true!—the young captives extended and continued the myriad cracks which webbed the glass. The jagged fissures followed erratic patterns through foreheads and eyes, noses and chests, and one crack decapitated a tall, shy-looking girl with long black hair.

The fragmented sight of their own forms leaping through the bodies of these mirror children drove the Virbius men mad. It was doubly humiliating, since their futile activity with the wire cage found its own image on hairless chins and schoolboyish lips, on immature cheeks, fingers, eyelids and hands. The men had taken their cue from their Sergeant-at-Arms, and they wept. Several would not settle for unabashed tears. They sprang like tigers at their young captives. They could not tolerate the children who had slid into the mirror for preservation. A mob, the Virbius men beat at what they imagined to be warm, yielding flesh. They tore their hands open. The glass, now alloyed with a variety of youth, chipped only slightly under the attack. The men tried to tear away the imprints of the children from the face of the mirror. "You can't get at them!" I yelled from the balcony. "You can't get at them!"

One man held a hand high in the air, in plain view of the children: a prophet trying to produce an effect of horror. His hand was webbed, and the joining skin ran to the topmost joints, and not a single space showed between any two fingers. At this sign the children began to cheer, wave after wave of cheering, until their captors gave up and ran away. I managed to get out and into the street, where I hunted for and failed to find my friend Quastafesti.

TUESDAY

ॐ FOR SEVERAL WEEKS FOLLOWING THE VIRBIUS AFFAIR Vincent wanted nothing to do with me. The door of his shop was locked. We met on three occasions, in the hall and on the street. He was full of the subject of Virbius.

"After I fell off the stage," he said, on our first meeting, "I lost all hope. A fiasco! Did you notice the Wellerky boy? And the Costa twins? And Turino's little girl?"

"I noticed the Costa twins."

"And the eternal police! They'll hop in hot and cracking when what is really needed is a pail of water and a couple of mops. With their idiotic questions! . . . Well, what would they do with the facts, eh?"

And again, on Thirteenth, along the loading zone of the icehouse, as he leaned on his handtruck, by which he transported his cases of dolls to his Elizabeth Street jobber: "Too bad you didn't find me. You should've come to that cafeteria on Irving Place. You know . . . our cafeterias deserve an esteemed place in your city's life. Every empty headed *yut* in a cafeteria has a hand in our finest moments. Well, there's still Union Square when you come down to it. There you can find out what God is doing these days along with His economists! But the oratory isn't quite the same, is it? Too bad we tooted

out the old anarchists. People used to hemorrhage at
the mind on occasion, but no more! We've destroyed our
initiative for lyricism. That's where your disillusion
should lie, my belabored artist, in that loss of our dis-
tinctive passions. A pinch of sociology, a snip of physics,
a yellow pill or two to untangle our constipations—
that's all we've come to. But we made a good try that
night in the cafeteria, Barney—our debate on Virbius
rolled and heaved like the sea! And outside I could see
the squad cars plowing in from every direction, their
tracer lights shooting into the snow. You should've
heard the epic narratives from table to table. A new
cause for the disaster with every bowl of Yankee bean
soup! One—the city is mothered by plot: the gang was
a well-organized lot of truant hoodlums nurtured by
Fascist elements. Two—the Communists had a hand
in it, according to the Catholics. Three—it's the *lumpen*
proletariat revived, according to the Communists.— And
what do you think, Mr. Yago?"

He seemed bent on trapping me into an argument.
But I resisted; that is, I remained the listener.

"Life is not hideous, only my views on it are, is that
it, Mr. Yago? What are you smiling at? Well, let me tell
you something—I've acquired some knowledge of your
views through your work. Ah, your work! Your high
narrative in jagged motion! Now what was your aes-
thetic philosophy exactly? Let me see . . . your limp!
That's it! You limp, thereby limps your narrative! Motion not intrinsic to the events, but intrinsic to the nar-
rator as he moves through the events. Motion plotted
meticulously, as a locus for your limping promenade.
Your bits and jags of metal and chalk breaking off your
narrative . . . for that's how you walk your streets, eh,
Mr. Scrittore, by thrusts and mischievous dips! Hah!

Yago, you're bankrupt! I've always said it . . . here's the event, there's your narrative. Total strangers! Tell me, Yago, when posterity plots the motion of our lives as lines or curves, what shape will yours take?"

"Cotyloidal."

"I beg your pardon?"

"The cotyloid is the cupshaped socket of the hip-joint."

When we met next in the bastard light of our hall, he begged my forgiveness. "What's the matter with me?" he said, "I've been acting like the Holy Father again. Though I know you see right through me!" He reached for my hand, asked again for my forgiveness.

"Your craft is not the furthest thing from my mind. Believe me, Barney, believe me. It's too close, all too close."

But then, he turned the subject of my work toward another attack. "Why the hell do you build mighty cathedrals round the dirty tricks life plays on people? What do you know about life? Are you such a moralist? Oh, I know—I know—your craft is your index, your craft returns you to your true measure amidst the horrors of your city! *Ufa!* —Yago will take the furtive rat and transform it into art. Yago will make the exalted inversion, presto! —and turn rats to stars!"

He plunged a finger into my chest. A bitter and incredible gesture. His bitterness was drawn from his fatigue, from his contention with me, and, perhaps, from some stupefying memory of the Virbius disaster. I had never seen him more distressed. There, in Cahoon's light, I could have sworn that his hair had turned white all in a flash. And then, he drove a finger again into my chest and laughed.

"To hell with you, Yago! To hell with your disgust-

ing city and your disgusting watchdog eyes! Do you
think you're all I've got to worry about? You and
your goddamned stump and your ridiculous craft?"

When Zena Cudcik died, the door of his shop re-
opened, as though the subject of her death would prove
the bridge over our recent lapse.

And so, on this Tuesday night, after listening to his
views on Tartock, I sat by and watched him work.

His shop was alive with bugs, and mice, and with
good cause, since the meals, which his father brought to
him at midnight, were never finished or thrown away.
Thus the shop was a cavern of fossilized food. During
the hot months the flies came also; they came in black
buzzing blizzards. He once said: "I'm imitating Zeus,
do you get me? I send to Argos my punitive plagues.
And why not?"

In a different mood, he claimed to enjoy the company
of all living things, crawling or otherwise.

His casual way round his smaller colleagues made
him their ideal host. In contradiction, his butcher's block,
where he worked, was clean and mirror-smooth. All else
suffered the scabrous skin of fossilized food, of grit, of
roach-egg shale and mouse nibs. Boxes, bags, cartons
were jammed high on his walls, up to the ceiling: they
spilled into the saturnine light the shirtings of his saucy
fabrics. The floor rolled like a ship's deck, its grit moved
like an oozing sap, and the sap was rich with sawdust
chips, spilled, like surplus grain, when Quastafesti
rushed an order for dolls.

He attacked his work as if one day it would make him
rich. On an ancient Singer pedalpumper he seamed the
backs to the fronts, which he had previously cut from
remnant bolts of cloth. Into the pouches he stuffed the

filler, then stitched the heads, and bound them judiciously with a golden twine. He thumped them round with a small wood mallet. When they were sound and tight and quick for life, on went the eyes, noses, buttons, belts—the smiles, leers, frowns, fears. When he struck a singularly vivid image on a doll's face, he would keep it for himself, placing it on a long plank behind his butcher's block.

He dipped into history, into mythology, for his costuming. His reproductions were clever and accurate. He had a true eye for color, and it was always exhilarating to go along with him for fabric into Orchard and Grand Streets. He would finger a piece of cloth and say: "How about this for a line of Robin Goodfellows?—too dull for a spicy little household sprite? Ah—what about this one for Heracles on his trip into Hades?—a little too brilliant? Old Charon would probably have tossed our hero into the lake in an outfit made of this junk."

Vincent's approach to business was simplified, and somewhat anachronistic. He sold his dolls to a single jobber. The detail of his handiwork demanded a certain leisure and his slow pace was a discipline on those eternal temptations to enlarge his production. When he did speed up a consignment he did so bitterly.

"I keep my market in a state of perpetual balance," he said, "you don't know what this means to me. Any other way would be chaos! I would end up hanging myself! More more more! Produce produce! Get the beat of that word, Yago—produce produce . . . papop papop! Do you get it? It's the American heartbeat, an old Calvinist curiosity! One day you and I are going to wake up and find the East River and the Hudson joined under our beds—the Island sunk under our acquisitive lusts! I don't know what's held us up this far. Don't

kid yourself, Barney—we're plunging into a vast corporate economy; this is the final black horror, and I am
one of the last of the holdouts—me, Quastafesti, on the
corner of Tenth Street and Szold, the darkest rectum
of your city!"

He worked away in his private rhythms, weaving and
rolling on a runted stool, while he scooped and tamped,
while he talked about this and that, and then not at all.
The shop window had long ago cracked in half; its two
jagged panes were sunk in the rotting frames. On the
outside, the crisscross slatting, meant for support, was a
ridiculous Cahoon expedience, and any breeze caused
a clash between the slatting and the glass.

Vincent settled an Italian curse on Cahoon's head, for
the man had kept the boiler cold most of the winter.
Vincent was galled by Cahoon's complicity with our
landlord: "It's the most poisonous relationship human
beings can have. How does a man become such a toad?
What dirty nightmares he must have! I've got an
eighty-year-old father, I've got poor Gilda. . . . Don't
they qualify for a bit of warmth now and then?"

And, in a moment, when I could not answer him,
he said: "Barney, listen to me—no!—wait!—I've had such
dreams these last weeks!—stay with me—"

He stopped short, the fetal pouch of a half-stuffed
doll in one hand, his grain scoop in the other. Outside there was a pumping of legs through the hard
sponge of yesterday's snow. Arab was out again, barking on Szold Place. Our building's eternal fragrance
rolled through the shop on a cold draft. Sniffing,
wrinkling his nose in a mockery of Mrs. Osot, he
said: "Hull vurlt full ir'rotten konchur! —Good
Christ! —Get the whiff, Yago . . . it's the body odor
of the angel of God flying through your city! . . ."

Then, in a quick and powerful seizure, he brought his grain scoop down on the head of a doll, killing it.

"Oh!—the objects of my love!"

He shot off his runted stool. Anger took his face. Like a man in a large drawing, he waved his scoop in the air. He shook the mutilated doll at me.

"Who in hell d'you think you are? You make me sick, you pretentious punk! . . . Come on with your beloved stump and your noble craft! . . . Come on, you louse! . . . I'll show you your perfect metaphor for life!"

He flung the dead doll over his shoulder, and it hit the lightbulb, exploding it in a blue sizzle. Immediately he had a handful of my sweater. My stump rolled in its bucket. The stump sock snarled. A bullet entered, a trajectory of pain from the tip of a phantom toe to a point beneath my cheekbone. He was, by now, outside the door while I was still inside it, and the sweater was fierce between us.

I had flopped over the runted stool. With Vincent still tugging, my nose was deep in wool, my head in camphor fumes.

"Yago!—Yago!—the nearest land to the ship is bottom of the sea! . . ."

"Let go of me—what?"

"Hull vurlt full deaf people! . . ."

On the first-floor landing he released my sweater. I followed him because he was a different man. In Cahoon's special light he was aged, murky, more faceless with years than Bibber, or Cahoon, or even Zena Cudcik when I saw her at the last.

At his door, 2G, he said: "Mrs. Wellerky's husband Francis cherishes his compulsion to urinate in our buss-tops. Twenty-four arrests do not discourage the man. He will live to see the replacement of all our buses by a fleet of submarines!"

Then he drove his finger into my breast and said: "Mr. wiseacre storyteller Yago!"

The Quastafesti apartment had been spilled out of a large crate. The rooms were not laid out, but smashed together, as though the crate, torn free from its moorings in heavy seas, had burst against a bulkhead. Each room was either a step up or a step down. Corners and angles were flattened; whatever you touched had a bruise and dent. How had the old man and Vincent and Gilda survived the crush? On coming in you had to immediately sit and immobilize yourself, and tilt your brain continually to the varying tilts of the spillage.

A small bulb burned under a green-glass funnel. A peculiar glow seemed to emanate from within every single object, as though the object itself was the source for its own illumination. Vincent, the old man, Gilda, shone with a platinum iridescence. I looked at my hands; my own skin had this glow just beneath it. Here, in these utterly pauperized rooms, was nature's light—a white moon, a Mediterranean glow fresh with sealight, sweetened by Mt. Etna, by Palermo, by the lulling whispers of the Tyhrrenian Sea.

Nothing else burned but the single small bulb, and yet the three of them sat white and glowing in their peaceful, glowing rooms. Vincent quickly regained his rightful definition. I'm sure they had forgotten I was there! . . . They were enchanted by each other, by the coincidence of their presence in the same room. But I was outside this charmed circle. . . . This gentle sealit gleam had excluded me.

And then I saw that the light had an actual source! Behind Gilda stood an old chest of drawers with a backboard mirror. The right front leg was minus a caster. The chest leaned-to on a perpetual perch. Beside Gilda stood a small rolltop desk, its large mouth stuffed with papers and books. Behind the desk the old man sat. When I came into the room only his head was visible, for the desk had walled him off. When Vincent finally said: "You know my father, Barney," I went behind the rolltop to offer the old man my hand. He was seated on a low stool similar to the runted stool in Vincent's shop. He wore a gunnysack tied round by a length of electric wire. The sacking was crusted and gnarled. I saw what stood at the old man's knees and I immediately looked back at Vincent, who held a finger to his lips.

At his father's knees, on a makeshift stand of bricks, was a large wooden crate packed with ground ice. Several whole fish and several more in parts lay on this frozen bed. So this was the source of the Mediterranean gleam! Under the small bulb in the greenglass funnel the ice glimmered and sparkled. The fish, too, in their fluid tonalities, lay in a lake of colors. And so the backboard mirror, tilted high over the rolltop, reflected the cold clean tones, casting back into the room this platinum iridescence of ice, this natural moon!

"Sit down, Barney," the old man said. During my stay those were his only words. There was no resemblance in him to either Vincent or Gilda. He had a small gray beard, proud, somewhat impudent—a miniature spade. His skin was flaked with dry fishscales. Little black bubbles of fishblood rode his perfect beard. A small chopping block stood at his thigh; a

wide knife, a scaler, a knife club, lay on the ice
near his hand. Altering his display of fish, he had the
air of the busy fishdealer, hooking two fingers under a gill. He held several fish up in the light so
that Gilda, his only, and eternal, customer, might
examine them. She disapproved of all his stock. He
then, craftily, scaled and split-quartered a carp and
held up each part to his daughter. Again she disapproved.

"Look at her! . . . She's being the expert. . . ." Vincent whispered. "She never buys. In fifteen years she's
never bought a thing!"

I leaned back in my chair.

This game, in which the old man and his daughter were locked, and Vincent too, if only as a spectator
(and as the man who maintained the daily provision
of ice and fish) had been going on for fifteen years!

"Listen," he whispered, "what you see is simple
enough! We're humoring a child's mind! Look at
her, my beloved Gilda! She's ten minutes older than
I am! We were brought up in a room behind the
old man's fishstand down on Water Street. He's a
weak, quiet old creature and this Water Street—it was
your city's first assault on us. The first which aims
at ready flesh. As for the spirit, my mother died one
day after we were born. Look at the old man! . . .
He's an illiterate, but he'd butcher you with that
knife if you touched a single paper on my desk!"

The crate was tilted. The ice melted through a
forward seam into a bucket underneath. Gilda stood
up now, unmindful of my presence, and jabbed her
finger into the bits of dripping fish held out for sale.
These rejected, the old man slapped them down on
the bed of ice and held up others. She rejected each

part in turn, and the old man went through his entire stock over and over. He knew his business well,
but she knew hers. Without a word uttered, by a
play of hands, a smile, he began to plead, to beg—
Please, please, buy this center cut—for a few cents
it's a beautiful piece of fish—

"Watch her," Vincent said, "look at her eyes . . .
how happy! We couldn't keep her at home until we
hit on this little scheme. She'd wander round for
days on end, down in the fish market, looking for
that little stand we lived with as kids. The old man
tells me she was bright as a kid, but I don't think
so. It must have something to do with me, the fact
that we're twins . . . I don't know . . . ah, I can't
remember her any other way. Watch her, Barney!"

"Papa!"

"She doesn't even realize you're here, Barney!"

"Papa!"

"Ah, she's on a mission, Barney—look at that offi-
cious grin!"

"Papa, Gretta Propish wants fish."

"She's buying for the neighborhood! A delegation
of one tough expert, self-appointed."

"*That!*" Gilda said. She pointed to half a carp. The
old man, in a fiction of pleasure and gratitude, wrapped
up the piece in newspaper. He put it aside.

"Mrs. Costa wants fish. *That!*" She pointed to a
strip of walleyed pike. The old man wrapped this
piece in newspaper and put it with the other.

"Yetta Nostrand wants whitefish." The old man
did as he was told.

"Mrs. Tartock wants *that!*"

As he wrapped each selected part in turn, the old man

grew more and more obsequious, shortening before my eyes.

"Mrs. Puente wants fish. Arab eats fisheads!"

She bought, after proper scrutiny and decision, fish for Mrs. Wellerky too, and August Turino's wife, and Mrs. Bramovitch, the butcher's wife. She bought and bought until the old man's stock was depleted. Suddenly, loudly, she said to the fishdealer: "Yutchie Helm is dead!"

"Ah, she's done it!" Vincent said.

I leaned toward him. "Done what?"

"She dares not conclude the sale. It feeds on status quo. The old man has always been a miserable bust—he must be denied even a penny sale. Don't you see? With all this neighborhood shopping she's teasing him on a grand scale. And when she uses news of a death, it's cruel. It's dramatic. It obliterates her commitments. Yesterday she used Zena Cudcik!"

Gilda stood opposite the old man, the crate between them. The old man waited. Then, with a quick force, Gilda clenched her hands and brought them joined down on the pile of wrapped fish.

"Junk!" she screamed. *"Shit!"*

She kept the club of her fists coming down on the pile again and again, until paper, fish and ice were mashed into pulp.

She stopped, and sat down. There was no further sign of her emotion. A ghost in her mind had tapped her shoulder, and called her away. The fishstand ceased to exist. But the old man knew this game must be of a piece! He raked through the icebed with a small metal claw, cleansing the ice of the pulp of his daughter's fancy. Tomorrow is another day. He stuffed the waste into a garbage bag. He packed the ice down solid,

worked it smooth, covered the crate with a burlap sheet.
Then, free of improbity, he swept out his little store
with a pushbroom worn to its wood, and he closed up
shop for the night. With one finger he lightly touched
Gilda's hair as he walked by her into the other room.

"Our God and we are His children," Vincent said.

I rose to leave.

"Hummocks and hucklebones," he said, "chase the
proud cripples."

"Vincent, I'm going."

"Stay. Excuse my tears. They're not for them, they're
for me! Stay, goddam you! Watch her, Barney, . . .
watch us!"

I sat again, with my eye out for quick access through
the clutter to the door.

"She'll come out with something!"

Gilda sat perfectly in a straightbacked chair, a tattered
ottoman at her feet. Across her lap was draped a handtowel, through which she kept putting a threadless needle. Her finger was tipped with a red cigarband, which
she used for a thimble. She laughed, gratified by the
progress of her invisible tapestry. Several times she inter-
rupted her work to look at her brother. On the ottoman
lay a deck of cards and several tarnished spoons. While
her needle hand was busy, the other kept placing one
spoon, then another, on her deck of cards. She took
great care to prevent the spoons from touching. Each
spoon was placed precisely in the position of its predecessor, which she lifted off the deck with a delicacy that
was surely a mockery of itself. Over each, as it was lo-
cated, she chanted: "One and two, two and three, three
and four, *rest!*" And off the spoon would come. Over
each her justice was pure and methodical, so that all

spoon destinies were identical. As she achieved style
with her spoons, and with her invisible tapestry, she
weaved and rolled, and her rhythm was that of Vincent's, when he scooped and tamped his filler into those
brightly colored pouches.

The room was cold with an oily coldness. It stank
of fish. Vincent blew into cupped hands; he sat crouched
in his chair, a heap of bad luck. Gilda's perfect posture
remained unchanged. She wore only a white summer
frock, and was barefoot. Her ears were pierced with
tiny gold rings. From the hall and street there came intermittent cracks of noise. Vincent, inconsolable in this
lethal cold, again settled a curse on the poisonous Cahoon. Gilda, so poorly dressed in white, so busy with
her mysterious techniques, was heedless of her brother's
cursing, of the smell, of the cold. She went on and on
with her needle, her spoons, and her deck of cards.

Then, I heard her say: "My mother—"

"Aha! She's out with it!"

"My mother, your father—"

"Aha—my beautiful Gilda. Nothing aimless in that
girl's head, Yago. *Listen* to her."

Vincent rose quickly.

"Watch me, Yago!"

Gilda drove her threadless needle into the ottoman.
She threw her handtowel to the floor. Her invisible
tapestry had ceased to exist. She flung her spoons in pairs
against the rolltop desk. Again a ghost had come by, to
tap her shoulder and call her away. Her precision remained, and she now brought it to bear on the deck of
cards. One by one she lifted the cards, showed them to
Vincent, and put them on her lap.

"King of diamonds!" Vincent called to her. "Three of
clubs! Nine of hearts!"

Gilda began to chant: "My mother, your father lives across the way . . . two fourteen East Broadway . . . every night they have a fight . . . it's dirty what they say!"

Coming forward, Vincent plucked off the cards that lay on her lap and put them into the deck, which he quickly had taken out of her hands. Opposite the chest of drawers, he could view himself in its tilting mirror. He held his hands up to quiet her, to divert the force of her child's song. (And through my mind passed a memory of that Virbius man, who had held his hand up high, in plain view of those captive children, that hand so hideously webbed.) The backboard mirror cast a performer's spotlight over Vincent's imaginary stage.

"Gilda, my darling, . . . look, . . . look here!"

I called to him. He did not hear me. Muted squeals came out of Gilda's throat. Her ecstasy was vindication enough. He held the deck of cards up high, and, with one hand, worked a series of spectacular fanfares and spreads. Then, from somewhere (from his desk, I think), he produced a simple ruler, and he placed it on the index finger of his right hand. The finger became the ruler's fulcrum and the miniature seesaw teetered freely. With a flourish he placed the deck of cards on one end of the ruler, and nothing on the other. It all remained in balance!

"Gilda, . . . this deck of cards is weightless. You see, my love? Here, here, I'll show you how it's done! It's the key card sliced to make the prop, . . . you see? It's the injog and the undercut! Gilda, . . . this is the famous trick that defies every known law of physics! It surpasses the work of Jean Eugene Robert-Houdin. It's supreme! It destroys Verbeck! Bellachini! Maskelyne! Casaneuve! Gilda, . . . Gilda, . . . who is greater than Imro Fox?"

She sprang from her chair. She brought her hands to her mouth to trap her screams. She passed both hands over her face, her arms. She caressed herself. She anointed her skin with her own wild sounds. Before her brother's consummate art she began to handle herself, to fondle her breasts. She coveted her thighs, her buttocks, and was unable to stop this spree on herself! Vincent kept on with his weightless cards. She reached for him.

"Now me!—me too!—me!—me!—"

I remember, clearly, the cards, the ruler, flying from his hands. I remember, too, the old man coming into the doorway of this tiny room to stand there in silence. He lightly fingered his perfect little beard. No longer a player in this game, he was free, by consent of all, to see to its arbitration. But his insinuation into the doorway was so tacit, so withdrawn, that it had the effect of a still slide passing onto a screen in a somber, echoing hall. The movement of his hand to his beard was the thing which caught my eye. I do not remember how Vincent vaulted the clutter to embrace his sister. But, as her own hands were just this minute stilled, Vincent began to create an effigy of his sister's spree on her own flesh. He faithfully reproduced her extravagance. His hands moved powerfully and fast over her body, yet not outdoing hers. Taking hold of her from behind, he pressed his mouth into her neck. Gilda tore at her white summer frock. I got up and fought the clutter to get away. As I turned to reach for the doorknob, I caught sight, in the tilting backboard mirror, of the track of a tear down a bared and glowing breast.

WEDNESDAY

ॐ ON WEDNESDAY NOON CAHOON KNOCKED AT MY DOOR, wild with hope. We spoke for an hour. I gave him my word to meet him that night at the Republican Club on Avenue A. There, I would talk with Ippilito.

Had the hard sponge of snow remained, I would not have gone, since my limb, in snow, will not plug along properly. But the day had warmed and a heavy rain had come, clearing the streets. By nine o'clock it was cold again, and misty.

When I arrived both Cahoon and Ippilito were late. The club was a huge room, four flats broken through, above an outlet for dayold Dugan's. The place had an air of deliberate denudation, as if here, between four straight walls, stood a common confessional.

Gathered round several tables were a dozen Republicans, deep in cribbage, in pinochle. I recognized Aza Luft and August Turino and John Helm. Their peddler carts had left them tarred and tough. Now they were having a good time. The bladegrinder seemed transfigured, as if a new energy had come to him since Yutchie's death.

"Barney Yago! Welcome to our club!"

"Thank you, Mr. Helm. . . . I'm waiting for Cahoon."

"He's been out with Judge Merchant all day."

Helm had lost much weight since the death of his son. His jaw had lengthened, his ears stuck out, his frame was angular. With this new energy, his brooding air was gone, though something of the hawk, the neighborhood stalker remained.

He stood up, quite abruptly. Cupping his hands round his mouth, he bawled out: ". . . Inlanders all! . . . from lanes and alleys, streets and avenues . . . landsmen all! . . . pent up in lath and plaster, tied to benches, clinched to desks! (pushcarts to you, you bums!) . . . inlanders all! . . . are the green fields gone? . . . from north, east, south and west . . . yet here we all unite! . . ."

Aza Luft, Turino, and the fourth man at their table, sat as if surprise naturally bred suspicion.

"That's Herman Melville," John Helm said to them. "I used to read him to Yutchie every night. It was the only thing could quiet the poor kid and put him to sleep. Some wonderful man!"

Helm put his hand out to me. Then, he comically pinched his own cheek, and said: "Do you think you're dealing with a nobody?"

"An actor," Aza Luft said. "Go on, John—give us some more."

"In the line of what?"

"Anything," Turino said.

"For God's sake—you're an actor!" the fourth man said.

Helm walked several paces from the table.

"Go on—go on!" Aza Luft said.

Helm looked first at me, then at the others, and gave out a boyish laugh. The Republicans round the other rocking tables were, by now, drawn to the spectacle of Helm's newfound prominence. They turned in their chairs, waiting for him to proceed.

"I'll give you something Yutchie loved!"

Helm looked ceilingward, kept his gaze there, as if

to search out some lingering overhead threat. He pointed his finger in the air, with such style that I expected him immediately to say: "A lesson in comparative prose readings, read from memory!"

"Jack London," he said. "Quastafesti the dollmaker gave me his books to read. So—Jack London. '. . . The streets were filled with a new and different race of people, short of stature, and of wretched or beer-sodden appearance. We rolled along through miles of bricks and misery (Jesus!—make that squalor!), through miles of bricks and squalor, and from each cross street and alley there lurched a drunken man or woman. . . .' "

He had stopped.

"To hell with it! —Come on, this is foolish, deal the cards!"

The hall resumed its straight-walled stillness.

"He was talking about London, England," Helm said, "and then it goes on about some children dancing round a garbage Maypole."

"Fancy that," Cahoon said, who'd entered softly from behind in his characteristic tread, to witness Helm's public moment unnoticed. His back was to a wall, his elbow touching the large pole-hung American flag, and, rising in a flat column behind his head, were the framed portraits of current party functionaries. He winked at me; whispered: "Imagine the hidden depths to the man! Helm's father, y'know, prayed for twins. So John showed up—with two personalities."

"Look who's here," the fourth man said. "Mr. Cahoon."

"Himself," Cahoon said. He moved quickly away from me.

"It's Mr. Cahoon all right. In the flesh," the fourth man said. "Pretend it isn't."

"Ah—them three famous words we'll chisel into your headstone, Mr. Eggcandler. *Pretend it isn't.* There's your life, don't y'know. Pretend it isn't. Levy the stone man, down on Suffolk, would be tickled silly to do the engravin' free of charge. *Pretend it isn't.*"

Cahoon turned to me.

"Do you happen to know the eggcandler, Mr. Yago? He's the royal pretender, y'might say. Now we've all got to help him keep up appearances. Isn't that right, eggcandler? Now pretend we're all at the Union League Club. *Um ganzer bunch.*"

"Pretend you're the President," the fourth man said. "With your dirty hags in the cellar. And your landlord."

"Pretend I'm not," Cahoon said. "I'm talking about Life. Pretend it isn't. You're an *egg*candler! Locked in a three-inch hole in the wall by a black curtain for your— how many cents an hour? Justify *um ganzer zach!*"

"Better a black curtain than a landlord's tongue!"

"Hah! Hah!" Cahoon put his hand over his brow. "Pretend *um ganzer veld* you're not just another little egg walking through your own fingers—your sensitive genius fingers! Hoorah the pullet, hoorah the hennery brown! —Now it's a concatenation, wouldn't you say? Marching, marching, one by one—by the dozen, by the filler, by the crate and coupled car! By the goosy goddam gozillions! Hah! Look at the man, Mr. Yago— poised on his own fingertips up to the miserable beacon! Pretend your eye isn't keen on yourself, eggcandler, for the fault and the flaw, the bloodspot and the floatin' chick!"

"Pretend you're not just a dirty beer guzzler with a cellar full of dirty hags!"

"Pretend you're not an eggcandler! Pretend you don't pretend your precious eggs will save you yet! Christ be

with us! —The machine has come! You're done in, eggcandler, a thousand eggs to one!"

"With a dirty prejudiced janitor's mind!"

"Um ganzer fliegel—hah!"

"Pretend!" the eggcandler said.

"Pretend!" Cahoon said. "Fellow Republicans, . . .
pretend the eggcandler isn't out on bail for public ma-
nipulation of his private parts!"

I had never before seen the eggcandler. He was
shorter than Cahoon, heavier, with a kindly, intelligent
face. He had the soft, pinkish skin of the non-shaver. He
was the only man in the Club who dressed in a formal
suit, shirt, and tie. In his mouth was a dead cigar.

Aza Luft, Helm, and Turino, at their table, toyed with
their hands, their chins down in a hopeless way, as if
once again disaster was only a word away. The men at
the other tables faked concentration in their games. The
eggcandler sat staring at Cahoon, who, standing behind
Turino, simply stared back. Everything about the eggcandler took on a twisted look. He now appeared dwarf-
ish, dressed in the clothes of an enormous man. His
breathing was rapid. He began to sweat. His dead cigar
rode round his mouth.

The Club, all this time, had been filling up with petitioners seeking an audience with Ippilito. I did not notice the influx because my attention was so strongly fixed
on Cahoon. They had come in so quietly; one by one the
available camp chairs were taken up. With Ippilito not in
sight they sat by quietly and waited. Mrs. Bramovitch,
the butcher's wife, had come to report on her husband's
stroke, and to inquire about the delay in arrival of her
welfare checks. Propish was there, with his wife Gretta,
to squash a subpoena for jury duty. Victor Puente was
there for a job, and to complain of the rats in the walls

of his baby's room. Beside him, in her eternal white shoes and bright cream dress, sat the inconsolable Yetta Nostrand, who, for the past two months, had visited the club nightly, to enlarge on the appalling arrogance of our city's roving hags, some of whom had come into her shop for corset fittings. Gina and Doris Zwar, the two knitting sparrows of Avenue C, were there to augment her. Of the petitioners least apologetic, the least apologetic was Mrs. Osot, enlarging on her prayers for our lungs' salvation. Costa, the woodworker, came to buy off a traffic summons, half-price. Marks, the candy and nut man, had come protesting antagonistic decisions of our neighborhood's rent commission. Mrs. Tartock, whose husband's night hours often confused her, had come too, in the thought that it was Thursday, hence bingo night. She was accompanied by Mrs. Wellerky, a woman who, despite her own hard life, possessed a perfectionist's grip on the calendar, but who periodically would close her newsstand a bit early, to observe firsthand how Mrs. Tartock could hang herself by her own perplexity. Arab had come by, sniffing for his master, and was kicked down the stairs by Mrs. Bramovitch, who tolerated only cats on this planet. With the exception of Yetta Nostrand, all were strangely still; they just sat and waited and stared at Cahoon.

Though motionless, Cahoon was acute and expectant, perched at right angles over the eggcandler's forthcoming provocation. Somehow, he had twisted his glass eye from its socket. The eye-cave was now covered by the familiar denim patch. He managed the change unnoticed, and as the eggcandler shot up from his chair, Cahoon pulled off his black scurfy hat, crushed it, jammed it into a back pocket. From his workjacket he pulled a Legion cap and put it on at a cocksure angle.

"Yankee Doodle Dandy!" the eggcandler sang out. He shook his fist at the janitor. "Do you think you scare me, you dirty janitor?" Then, with all the parody he could muster, he puffed himself up and saluted Cahoon.

"Eggcandler! Oh, eggcandler!" Cahoon yelled. "Oh, Child of Israel! Where were you when I earned the right to wear this cap? Where were your three sons when Yago here buried his leg under German soil? Oh, eggcandler! Where are your wrathful warlike generations of David? *Duvid'l! Um ganzer* punks! Hah! Oh, Zone of Interior! Oh, Quartermaster! Oh, Special Services! How is it Yago here was suitable fodder? Is it his blue eyes?— his flaxen hair?—his *goy* nose?"

The eggcandler was enthralled by the movement of Cahoon's mouth. Then, he turned away. He walked to a wardrobe locker marked RECREATION, at the furthest end of the hall. There, he dug into the locker and came up with a pair of boxing gloves. He undid the laces, tossed one glove to Cahoon, who caught it, put it on, then put it forward to John Helm, who tied the laces round. None of the others made a move to stop them! The eggcandler now went toward Cahoon, and they faced each other, one hand gloved, one hand bare!

Unexpectedly, Cahoon turned round to me.

"Look at the man, Yago! Hah! In bed every night at ten o'clock, with his long underwear!"

The next thing I knew was this: Cahoon rushed through the Club's rear exit and was followed by the eggcandler. One by one the others went too, and I followed last.

We went down the one buckling flight into a cellsized inner court. Round us four tenements rose; we were a mob in an ancient tower, mailed and moated.

The court's center drain had clogged under the heavy

daylong rain. We sloshed in water ankle-high. Cold fog plumed the battlements six floors up. A dozen heads, like bowls on a shelf, idled on a roofledge. A yellow nightlight burned in the small back window of the dayold Dugan's store. An incandescence, pale and greenish, issued from a lighted bedroom here and there, a kitchen, a toilet. It was sufficient for us to see by. Because of the cold an icy sludge was the universal skin; whatever you touched had a mudsoft goiter. Windows flew up, heads popped out, some fire escapes served as galleries. On others, lumpy piles rose up in dunelike desolation. An Olympian net of clothesline seemed to be moving down on us, lowered by a great and mischievous hand. We scuffed and kicked in the ankle-high lake, where an armada of hundreds of bits of things raced and rammed, from greenpea pods to syrup jars.

From the roof someone unloosed a counterfeit snowfall. Miniature banks grew up on sills. Newspaper flakes floated into open windows, from which a babble of dialects toppled down.

"It's been going on for years," John Helm said. "This eggcandler has been putting a bug into Cahoon's ear that his wife Esther is hot on Bibber, a neighbor of yours, and Bibber has a yen for her too! True or not, these two'll never quit plucking each other's feathers out!"

Helm wheeled to his duties after telling me this. He ringed people back upon the walls, clearing an arena. He too was transformed!—no longer a boyless father of minutes ago, but a giant of authority, whose very bulk restored our vanities after having first abduced them. We were now an almost perfect circumference of spectators, for Helm's admonitions on the importance of a clear arena had an immediate effect. Within the circle stood Cahoon and the eggcandler. Directly above my

head a Puerto Rican boy was halfway out a groundfloor
window. He laughed, and I turned to look up at him.
The boy offered his hand. I shook it gladly. His excitement was no less than mine.

"Gino—" he said.

He had an open smile, small, dark, lively eyes. There
were several gray welts on his neck and face, a faint scar
on his temple. And the little hand that I shook was also
scarred. But these blemishes did not disfigure—they
seemed to perfectly fit him.

I wanted to talk with him, though I knew he was ignorant of English, but Cahoon and the eggcandler were
already at each other. It began as I turned round to shake
the boy's hand.

"Keep clear of the pit!" John Helm yelled to an old
woman, who had stooped to pluck an abandoned shoe
out of our ankle-high lake.

Cahoon, taller than his enemy, bent forward stiffly, trying, seriously, to shorten himself, to equalize the contest.
Both arms were tight to his sides. His workjacket collar
was up; its points stabbed at his ears. His hands were
fast on his thighs. Was their use prohibited? He splashed
forward, he spit at the eggcandler, dunning him to battle. He broke the line of his body's slope while the eggcandler tried to push himself upward to a fighting
height. But the man was not bred for this effort.

Their rigidity, their downright refusal to lift their
hands, their splashing and circling, the futility of each
with a single glove, their apparent concern to equalize
heights before touching each other—it was all pathetic
and doltish! Helm circled round them. It was plain that
he'd been a referee to this bout before!

They wheeled and gawked and wagged at each other,
armless. Suddenly, the eggcandler jerked, his spindle

legs snapped, he would have pitched forward into the
muckthick lake, but he was caught and righted by the
bladegrinder, who then fished round and found the
tripping thing—the twisted skeleton of an umbrella—and
tossed it into a corner. This slight accident, this innocent
stumbling and Helm's intercession, shook the two men
out of their posturings. Cahoon lunged, his rump out,
his chin down, armless, his collar up, brisk as a clipped
hackle, his head a butt with a two-inch spur! He made
for the eggcandler's chest, to drive this imaginary spur
into the little man's heart!

The eggcandler took the blow without moving his
arms to defend himself. Heart pierced, wattle flapping,
he jumped into the air shrieking. Cahoon backed away,
poised for retaliation, and the other came at him in the
same strange way, rump out and chin down, armless,
hackle clipped, head a butt with a menacing spur, and he
made for Cahoon's chest—not, however, to butt or stab
it, but to tear at his clothes with his mouth. The eggcandler's mouth was a blazing beak!

"Bastard!" Cahoon said.

"Count his wounds!" the other said.

"Suck out the bastard's blood!"

"Count his dirty wounds! Make him sweat!"

"Throw the runt in a basket!"

"Throw the dirty janitor in salt water!"

In truth, neither had touched the other. There were
no wounds, nothing was torn; the attacks were bloodless. The deception lay in the fury of motion. The two
men flopped and cawed while the crowd exulted in their
impotence! They howled and hooted, flung things at
this ludicrous pair of shawlnecks.

Cahoon and the eggcandler were unable to imperil
themselves. Both were too devious for the pointblank

fight. Hate, thus betrayed, searched out sham effects, jigging on birdlegs in a counterfeit snow. So, in mockery of hate, Cahoon and the other were pitted to each other as fighting cocks.

Still armless, with beaks blazing, they wagged and cawed while the crowd exulted. They were breast to breast in the middle of the pit.

Helm splashed round like an Indian feeder.

"Bleed or you're dead!" he yelled. "Bleed or you're dead!"

And the crowd, resigned until now to the issue and outcome, began to act uneasily. A towel flew out of a window, a beercan, a candybox full of bottlecaps. Yetta Nostrand, her principality going wild before her eyes, picked up the umbrella skeleton and clanged with it on a groundfloor sill. A straw beach-hat from an upper-floor origin sailed down upon us. The bladegrinder was struck by an orange peel. By some miracle the center drain was freed, and our ankle-high lake receded. In minutes we were dry on a giblet beach.

Helm's position as arbiter was plainly self-appointed. He behaved, however, now that the crowd was unful-filled, as though he had invested too heavily in his rank. He was desperate now to be rid of it: there was an in-jury too unjust to sustain for another minute.

My new friend, Gino, with a random thought's leap and swiftness, came out of his window, to deposit him-self in the fighting pit. He was joined almost instantly by another boy who, it seemed, had been leashed in like a hound for the call, at the courtyard door of the dayold Dugan's store. Cahoon and his enemy dug round in their pockets and brought out dollar bills. Each boy was given one. Then, the janitor and the eggcandler removed their boxing gloves, and laced them round the hands of the boys!

The dollar bill in his pocket, his right hand comical in its oversized boxing glove, my little friend was beguiled by his own fitness to complete Cahoon's business in this courtyard. His smile grew brighter. The other boy (the eggcandler's main), less welted (but hired before), had a dark, serious face, and permitted himself to be prepared and handled without Gino's flourishes and wild laughter. Then John Helm, booming a depleted giant's call into a bizarre, singsong cadence, pressed the crowd back to the walls again, and cleared the eggcandler and his enemy out of the pit.

The two boys, with the bladegrinder's help, stripped to the waist despite the cold, their shirts and sweaters taken by their employers. Heeled to their jobs, they faced each other in a soft crouch, their gloved hands hip-high, their bare hands clenched and up to their chins, knuckle-white, each giving the other a ritual salute. They were waiting for some signal from Helm, and, though I did not see it, it came.

As the boys flew together and collided they were showered from the windows by pellets of fine white bread, as if the principal diet of true fighting cocks had been violated! But Gino was a true bird with beak in hire; he sank his teeth into the other boy's shoulder. Gino's ear was immediately opened; a patch was torn from his cheek. The pattern was clear. The other boy was commissioned to strike at the face, Gino the body, on the initial attack. Then their marks were reversed by intuitive consent, so that no advantage would be sacrificed.

Tiny ridges in a flooded field, Gino's welts were now

washed in blood. Like feathers, the blood flew off the boy-cocks. The vandalism of flesh would not relent. The crowd of petitioners, the tenement gallery, even Yetta Nostrand, grew quiet as savagery deepened. In minutes, repeated teeth strikes made pulp out of young flesh on brows and cheeks, on necks and chests. Sweat, in the dismal cold haze, gave a curious luster to the diminishing patches of skin still bloodless and whole. Where strikes missed, there were bruises, which seemed to be raised and depressed by a will of their own. With teeth striking and white, with dark blood running, with bruises shifting swiftly through an assonance of colors, and the feathers of blood flying, I could not tell who it was that fell, until I heard, "Gino!"

It was Victor Puente who called the boy's name. He knelt at the fallen Gino. He took the tricolored handkerchief the bladegrinder offered and dabbed at the bleeding face. He bent low and spoke in Spanish into the boy's ear. Gino moved his lips, and Victor Puente bent lower to catch the words. The other boy now went to his knees to join Victor Puente, and, as he stroked the wet pad of Gino's hair, I heard him say: *"El es carinoso."*

While bent to Gino's lips, Victor Puente began to pass his hands over Gino's body. His fingers worked swiftly over the flesh, and very soon, the nature of each wound was revealed to the crowd.

"Exactemente!" Victor Puente kept saying. *"Exactemente!"*

Gino lifted his head. *"Tiene el un lapiz?"*

"Si . . . si. . . ."

From an inner pocket of his jacket, Victor Puente took out a long yellow pencil. Calmly, he offered it to Gino's conqueror, who, very slowly, in conjunction with Puente's precise explorations, began, with the aid of this pencil, to count Gino's wounds. The blade-grinder subtly withdrew his influence, though I heard him counting too. Now relieved of his role as arbiter, he seemed pleased. As for myself, my heart was fixed on this long yellow pencil moving steadily, and restfully, from one wound to the next, for it seemed on this alone life's balance turned.

The pencil moved steadily, dutifully, one, two, three, four, each wound impeding, for an instant, its forward motion, and at each another spectator, himself impeded by the steady dousing of tenement lights (until there was a blind press at the foot of the one buckling flight of stairs), left the court.

PART TWO

PART TWO

WEDNESDAY

INCHES IPPILITO WAS NEVER IN FEAR OF A SOLEMN truth, nor of a punitive judgment. Nor did he suffer the tradition of mutable effects. Since the peregrinations of his geese were infinite, untraceable, he had, properly speaking, no face, but an historical smile, a glidepath on which to send his petitioners winging.

His smile was worked with care, elevated in the style of a bas-relief; he wore it as a clasp for a man's belt, as a medallion round the neck, as a pin for a lady's breast, as a ring for a child's hand.

Judge Merchant, who had arrived with the captain, and who stayed at his side while the petitioners were dealt with, had, properly speaking, only a face, nothing else. Sometimes, by a quick theft, he reproduced on his own blank medal a measure of the excellence of Ippilito, our neighborhood's master smilesmith.

The Judge, when chipping at the block of the East

Side Jews, was oiled by a public aphorism: Merchant, on the bench a *mench*.

Dapper, highcollared, powerfully cuffed, he was given, in this day and age, to sleeve garters, to button-hole sprouts and piped lapels, a magnifying glass on a ribbon, a platinum chain and pendant, Melachrinos, a snuffbox under a seal of justice, breath sweeteners, an Indian head on a quadrangular ring, fingernail moons and bayrum, tweed spats, three-fingered handshakes, benevolent obscenities, burrless slogans, an antipathy for the wits of Clinton Street, tickers in poolrooms, and ex-temporaneous courtroom eclectics. The Judge was also fond of the Industrial Revolution.

Inches Ippilito, on the other hand, was given only to his smile, and to his ever-present flask of whiskey.

Mrs. Osot was the final petitioner. She first thanked Ippilito for these repeated opportunities to put her case before such high authority. She then, briefly, reminded her captain of her husband's konchur. She then, labor-ing at length, evaluated her position in relation to the breathable elements of our city's atmosphere. Ippilito concurred in her theory of our lungs' ustulation. He em-braced her. With a progression of referrals to Judge Merchant (in the interests of judicial sonority) he in-formed her of an injunction issued this very day upon Consolidated Edison in the citizens' crusade against air pollution.

Mrs. Osot was willingly lifted onto the glidepath of her captain's smile (properly holding her skirts) and was shot home in gladness.

Judge Merchant all the while had been scanning the East Side News with his magnifying glass, pinky ex-tended. Without lifting his head, he said: "Function or stand aside, Ippi. To behave like a cow is to, you'll pardon me, piss on the rocks. Don't you think that woman is a walking nostril? Quivering into the bargain? Is it not advisable to send her to an ear, nose, and throat man?"

The Judge gave a little cough.

"I had it in mind, Judge. *Ma-rone!* What can you do with such a nut?"

"Crack it. Tell me, does she sneeze her ballot into the voting slot?"

"She's always on time with her rent, Your Honor," Cahoon said. "Faithful. That counts for a lot. Like Barney Yago here."

"To be sure. I would nevertheless remand her to a specialist."

On the stout side, Judge Merchant, perspiring out of season, polished his reading glass with a large linen, snapped it into its blackbone shell, dried his brow and neck, and spread the linen out square on the table, to dry.

"Felonious business, this cancer," he said.

"Sad all round," Cahoon said.

"Well, say—though she's my tenant, she's still a human being."

So this was my landlord! Judge Merchant, the old-fashioned absentee!

He turned to me and offered his hand. I took it indifferently. A weak welcome. I was drained from the courtyard business, which, for the three now present, especially Cahoon, had been dismissed from mind and memory. But what had happened to little Gino?

So: I stood up. I pointed a finger first at Ippilito, then at Judge Merchant.

"I'm ready. What's your proposition?"

Ippilito looked at my mouth. I resisted a persuasive hoist onto the glidepath of his smile. The Judge-Landlord, threatening a smile himself, again extracted his magnifying glass, and, with his great wet linen, wiped away the yellow fog of my brass tacks. Cahoon, beside me, in a new voice from, it seemed, the back of beyond, said: "I spelled out none of the details for Mr. Yago. It wasn't my place, Your Honor."

"Well, say, Mr. Yago—" the Judge-Landlord said. "May I in passing relate a little tale by way of introducing ourselves? Your grip on the bull's horns I find commendable, and at this hour of the night, taking account of our recent excitement in our, ah, courtyard, even advisable. But, you know, only a short while ago I buried an uncle. A mean man. A tyrant. A father who ate his children—my cousins—alive. A husband who reduced his wife—my aunt—to three spots of chalk on the wall. Now in the tempest, the whirlwind of his departure, he was buried in the wrong plot, the right *cem*etery but the wrong plot, not the width of a grassblade removed from an ex-changetaker for the old West End line, now an elevated—are you a Brooklyn boy?—it used to run on the surface of Bath Avenue. The man was murdered in 1927 by a gang of, with all due respects, greaseballs. Now this changetaker, it was soon divulged by a crack team of investigators, was a gang member himself who defected from a plan to rob his station. Ah, these bewildered Latinos! So—an uncle to Judge Merchant shoulder to shoulder with a criminal! *Requiescat in Pace*. I wonder do the maggots undress the corpse before dining? But what about those three spots of chalk on the wall: namely, my aunt? Well, my son, the spots deepened, and grew, and spread at such a speed that they wheeled off the wall entirely, not two hours after the tyrant was mislaid in the ground. So loud she was, so full of rage, so enjoined by her desire for fair play, that, miracle of miracles, *she* became *he!* Well—I'm in the position of having lost an aunt by burying an uncle. You see? Whom do I grieve for?"

"So you've had it from Mr. Cahoon that I listen and never ask questions!"

"From Mrs. Cahoon, too, in the bargain. Ahh, what is our curse? To outsmart nature at every turn? Our laws aren't written that way! And what do the scriptures tell us?—profit ye all by the yea and the nay of it!"

"I'm anxious about your proposition, Judge, if one exists."

"Not that I like to see my colleagues reduced to an irreducible minimum. I mean, isn't it advisable to roll things along on a first-name basis? Oh, I've seen young hopefuls overplay modesty, and do it badly; why, I've seen myself working hand in hand with a stitch in the upholstery, a sticker on a windshield, a tooth in a zipper, no eyes, no senses, no passions, a puff of smoke, a draft of air, a zero, a nothing! Who needs it? I like you better—but slowly, slowly."

"Are you a registered Republican?" Ippilito asked me.

"I do not vote."

"There's no room for moodiness," the Judge-Landlord said. "The Party is not that strong!"

Ippilito, all the while, had been nipping from his silver flask, and returning it to an inner pocket. Once, he grandly showed it to Cahoon, who, in turn, showed it to me, and, judiciously, I admired the engraved mad bull bursting through a knot of leaves. When Ippilito heard my stand on voting, he took a long swallow. Dramatically, he swelled, like an asp.

"Brehh, oooops, heh, tight shoes, so solly, solly, Thirty-eighth and bee wubbloo y, corner northeast. Campaign headquarters. Some location. Two paira pants. Full right rudder, old steward, *gegen z linx!* Unt vots mit doze cuffs?"

"Neither fancy nor plain," the Judge-Landlord said. "We must be broadminded, just broadminded."

"Let us roll!" Ippilito said. He stood up now. The Judge-Landlord also stood. They linked arms. "Roll, I say!" Ippilito yelled. "And I don't mean do it to a collar, Duke, or serve it with seeds, nor play it with a paira drumsticks. *Ma-rone!"*

Cahoon jumped from his chair, pulling at my elbow. "Jesus, aren't we lucky?"

Ippilito and the Judge-Landlord, facing me arm-in-arm, gave me the feeling that I was sliding out of myself.

"We need you, Barney Yago!" Judge Merchant said. "You're my silver cape caught full to the wind! Don't you forget, I'm a rare old coot with deep feelings! My umbrella is a matador's lance . . . have you ever seen me hail a cab? I've a set stance and a sure thrust! Something to behold in these toadish times. Picture it!   . . A night drenched in rain, *voluptuii ex metropole,* and the opera is out! Homburgs, toppers, coiffures, white scarves and purple faces, the golden moment, a metropolitan stew, limousines and mounted police! . . . In my hands the umbrella is a lance, long and deadly! Here comes a cab edging toward the curb, and it catches the upward arc of arm and lance, the pitch and roll of my form, the final true lunge! The driver is halted by a mortal wound, right between the eyes! He's mine!"

"Olé!" Ippi said.

"Moitzy gemocked!" Cahoon said.

"I'm a jack-be-nimble, Mr. Barney Yago, doing a pirouette on the hood of that cab to the tune of nickels dropping!"

"Flag up, Your Honor, it's an arm job all the way!" Ippi said.

"Ahhh, my dear Barney, . . . look at the company you're keeping, . . . but you, you, Barney Yago; who the hell can resist a one-legged veteran? You're the boy to make our dreams come true!"

"It's a gorgeous little opportunity," Cahoon said.

"Whatever you have in mind, I am not cheaply bought," I said to Judge Merchant.

"Ah, well, for the running length of the project a succulent forty-five a week."

"No good."

"Fifty."

"No good."

"Well, as the man who lost his plates says, *pifty-pive*. Highest we've ever gone!"

"It's a deal."

Hands were clasped all round. The flask passed from mouth to mouth.

"Highest we've ever gone!" Ippi echoed.

Cahoon bent low down, curiously, perhaps to vent his joy. His ambitions for me had been realized. He plucked crushed butts off the floor, and, as hands became full, Judge Merchant undertook to outline and explain the nature and order of my duties. Ippi, nearby, contributed an exact catalog of names, dates, facts, figures, hostilities and suspicions already in force. Their scheme was lofty, visionary—yet earthbound and workable too. I learned soon enough, yet much too late, that the aspirations of the schemers had little relation to those of the sovereign scheme, which was devised, with a realist's smirk at what's what (in view of the eternal separation between city government and populace), to humanize our neighborhood by means of plant and flower, to landscape our wretched valley. A tremulous vision, it was transmutable to the curb by the need of the people, implemented, of course, by their labor and money . . . which I was to induce and collect.

"The idea will catch on," Judge Merchant said, "it will gallop from street to street. They'll eat it up like so much popcorn. Our neighborhood a place of beauty, rolling banks of acacias and tiger lilies, big white mumsies kissed by rose leaves. From Avenue D to Avenue A, from the river, in fact, up to Third. I've given fifty dollars on my own to start us off. Advisedly, Ippi's keeping the books. He has charted the project in sufficient detail to withstand harangues and corroboration and, as our Jewish friends say, the most anti-Semitic of explorations. Our pavements a botanical garden! If there is nobody who cares—we do, we do. A few pennies from each of us, the trick is turned. From a goulash to a hanging garden, eh, my boy?"

"Yes, yes," I said. "As you know, I write. I will write our brochures and handcirculars, distribute them myself, from door to door, store to store, peddler to peddler."

"I was on the verge of that very thought," Judge Merchant said. "I could kiss old Cahoon for thinking of you were it not for his dirty fingernails."

"I will also plan the layouts on the bigger media, suggest the typeface. Is there a printer who is sympathetic?"

"We've a windfall of printers on Varick alone. Ippi will gather up their names and numbers."

"Could you advance me some money tonight?"

"Why not?" Ippi said. "Will a double saw do for a start?"

He gave me twenty dollars.

"Now in regards Mr. Kurl," Judge Merchant said, "our wholesale florist over on Thirty-eighth, he will underwrite the entire project, on, of course, an equitable return—he's a club member—and keep us in perpetual supply. He'll provide the caskets—ah, the chests, I mean—and all the rich loam to bed our gardens down. Block on block of pastel and almond caskets. Damn the people! What more do they want? They must kick in! Will the grubby pikers understand what we're doing?"

Maintaining what he thought to be eloquence, Ippi hurried along the walls switching off the overheads, saying: "Mr. Kurl is waiting on us right this mo, with you know what, Your Honor. No time like the present for old Barney here. Stick with old Barney here. Stick with the pattrin, Judge, the roll is hot. Don't fret the old noodle, Sir, I'm a studyin' fool on human nature. Judge, the action's here! It's here! Stick with the pattrin. Until old Barney showed, we been sittin' in the shade with our thumb in our mouth, now we're in basic industry. We always were a mother to the people, now we give 'em an older brother. Smart? Win or lose, old Barney's connectin' our hearts with a silver link. Judge, wait'll old Kurl with his soapbubble eyes meets our new exec— we'll no more sleep alone!"

"It was Esther my wife put you in mind, Mr. Yago, *she's* the one to be on it you're grateful at all. Lucy Tartock's got a fine-pointed needle out for you too, did

y'know that? And how about Rachel Bailey, the sodaman's wife? Lucy waitin' for the sun to come up to put
old Tartock to bed and you in her thoughts all the
while, and Rachel so quiet in her ways. You ought to
hear all their hellish blab!"

In the dark, as we moved toward the door in a lapse
of talk, Judge Merchant flourished his linen again to
give his nose a mighty blow. There in the vestibule between cracking walls, he sang. Ippi whistled. Cahoon
hummed. Or was it Ippi who sang, Cahoon who whistled, Judge Merchant who hummed? The dissonance
was joyous, for I had a job on my hands, sensible work
to do. The city had offered no better plan. Having
much to learn, I learned, in five minutes, that our money
vase sat on a broad, broad plinth. The people were certain to support the scheme! . . . Ippi and the Judge, together, exerted considerable influence over the day-to-
day services unifying our community: in one instance,
garbage collection. Already those who balked at con-
tributing were in danger of drowning in their own
putrid uncollected matter, of jail therefrom by city ordi-
nance, of pursuit by swarms of outraged neighbors. In
another instance: Judge Merchant and Ippi had more
than a shade of power in the Ninth Precinct; local
police protection, the quality of neighborhood enforce-
ment, was sensitive to unseen hierarchies. Rebels against
the small weekly payments forfeited the subsidiary
rights of civic benevolence, and were guilty of moral
obscenity, and uncivilness. They fed on the worms of
apathy and deserved the loathing of their friends.

The ride to Kurl was pandemonium, Ippilito its high
creator, ferrying us across his river of whiskey. The fog,

like sacred justice, caused Ippilito to lose his way. Time after time we circled Tompkins Square. East and north, west and south. At Union Square, a crack of thunder. North and west again. The city was depthless deep. We found ourselves on West Street once, blind under the eternal cap of highway el, truck enmeshed in roar and fume, great gears and great green bulkheads working by, ancient and pagan, Erie, B&O, Lackawanna, West Shore. Allnight diners too, hazy red eaters bestooled and countermouthed. Four policemen billy-linked, concealing their smoke from the Sergeant's car. Doorway hags, halted at a dripping sluice. Jerseyside crates, stenciled citadels. Clucking pigeon strays, yet unskewed. Rearwheel cats on cobblestones. The sweet Hudson yawping warnings. Wet pillars radiant. A fiddler, straddling his trouser seat, subsiding, uncomprehendingly, on a vacant corner, ascratch with molly and me.

"Got to give the captain his daily dozen," Cahoon said to me, in the back seat. "Worth it, worth it. It's a bonanza for Kurl, don't y'know. Just wait till you see how the man shows his appreciation. Hot's not the word for it. Jesus, it's a mad business."

We rode and rode, turning left, then left again. And now a freezing rain, now the fog, now an icy paste. A turn west, a turn north. Booted packers, hiphigh in slaughter. Calfbleats to an invincible commerce. Butchers letting blood, hosing a steaming mound of calfheads; eyes, tongues, hung out by cords, plucked by the city's claw of gluttony. We rolled our windows up, withdrawing from the stink.

"Phee!" Judge Merchant said. "I think the vegetarians have a bonafide point after all."

We were halted by a signal light. Happily, the calfcries and stink were behind us, the flopping hairlips, drooling. Judge Merchant took advantage of the respite and said to me: "And now for a bit of advice, Barney —now that you seem to be one of us. This Kurl might strike you prima facie like a strange duck. But don't conclude, my boy, don't conclude. Just go along, go along. Our project will make him. He's had a hard time of it through the years. Now what you might regard in the man as a bit of larceny, he regards as his birthright. There's much you'll agree imperfect in us all. Eat of the bread he offers. Why, in the nature of things it's clearly juridical. To be shy, or hesitant, or offended by his ways is to strike a threefold injury; to us, yourself, and nature. As Ippi often says, 'why spit in Mr. Washington's silky eye when it can't defend itself?' Kurl is our ace, my boy. In Ippi's own words, we were going to shylock this whole deal; that is, until the contributions came rolling in. Shylocks are a dirty breed. Why dirty up a simply wonderful idea? Kurl came to us by the will of Providence. If he prospers he also labors. He might prove to be a great man, all said and done. After all, what's closer to righteousness than to labor at our daily pain? You are a writer, my boy, and righteousness is an art, and we will imitate art because we are nature's babies. *Hein?*"

Money was the low country of our ascent. We four, Ippi's car, chattels in the climb. We went slowly into the rain's countersurge. Now and then a headless form convulsed through water sheets, titanic. One kept pace with us for half a block, ducking for a hiding place, a shaderoller in his hands.

"What the hell are we doing on Grand Street?" Judge Merchant said. "Turn on Allen; we'll make the lights."

"He's gassed," Cahoon said softly.

"Go learn me my city," Ippi said. "Go learn a priest his catechism!"

Angrily, he shot backward into Forsyth, reversed, and pierced north from there. The rain eased, easing our anxieties. Ippi, however, reminded of his excesses, sought new ways to torment us, sliding, veering, letting go of the wheel, jumping lights, raging wrong on wrong-way streets. Chrystie Street, half demolished: timber walks and walls. Broome, a long crabbed sentence: the city's unmetred mile. Lafayette (Go north! Go north!), fabric bales, tri-bellied, jamming a doorway: a silent flue to uptown fires. (An area of drift, imagine! This street a gneissoid agony; hard, hard Manhattan schist. The wooden dance of Esther Cahoon on feldspar, quartz, and mica.) Spring Street, lofts and jobbers careening: tenement ghosts. Ippi turned south again, spite empowered. Prince and Reade, driest of goods: a Burns nightwatchman for leather and hide. Where are the jewels of Maiden Lane? (Keep north! Keep north!) Astor Place, plateglass legends on goldleaf: a biblehouse too, incontinent in stone frisettes. (Keep north! Keep north!) Ah, have we no bells on our tires to warn the shades of the paupers of Wooster Street? (What are we doing here? North!) A saloon's charred shell, Cheap John's, two shots for one. Tap the horn lightly, lightly. Pawnk! Pawnk!

Ippi finally reached his Thirty-eighth and bee wubbleoo y, corner northeast. Kurl's place.

"His windows are dark," Judge Merchant said. "I wonder what's wrong?"

"It's been a coon's age I been this far north," Cahoon said. "I wonder what's new in the world? *Florence Sportswear*—that window is lit."

"Without doubt a couple of cleaning ladies," I said.

"Ah it's you, Mr. Yago," Cahoon said. "Jesus, I forgot you were still with us!"

"I think we're too late," I said.

Cahoon, thinking me annoyed, put a placating hand on my willow knee; awareness offended him. His hand jerked away, found refuge via his thumb and index on the lobe of an ear, again ventured toward offending knee, faltered, came to rest uneasily on my forearm.

"Mr. Yago—oh, I know it's none of my business, but how c'n I keep it down? Y'know, his honor's son is an editor in a grand old bookhouse. Might be there's a possibility the Judge'd break a few doors down. Might be it'd do you some good."

"Oh, yes," Judge Merchant said. "Oh, yes. It's been on my mind. Well, say—he's about your age, Barney, and a writer too. Ah, I don't presume he's gifted like you, but he's exceeding sympathetic. Though I haven't read your work, I've read all of his. Exceeding sympathetic. Can I arrange a meeting?"

"No. I thank you just the same. I don't mean to occasion any hard feelings. Let me put it this way: my work is a bridge between myself and the world, a single bridge which I've broken across my stump, as you would break a stick. . . ."

"Ah, say, that's not quite in my line."

Ippi, who had, on arrival, hurried from the car to investigate, now returned to us, holding a Manila envelope, which had been scotchtaped to Kurl's door, with a message.

"Dear Boys," Ippi read: "Why are you always so late? Do you have a few surprises up your sleeves? There are those who get impatient. I moved kit and kaboodle downtown, to the warehouse. You know where that

broken-down dump is, on Thomas, between Worth and
Duane. Lucky for me I don't pay by the hour! Don't
spare the horses!"

THURSDAY

ઠ્ AT THE WHEEL AGAIN, IPPI DROVE DUE SOUTH. IT WAS
after midnight. His silver flask ran dry.

"Don't spare the horses," he said. "Otza good! Otza
somma bum, ot somenobitch! Ooza e tink youenna me
weza be? Buncha somenobitchin cowboysa? O, otza
somma bum, ot somenobitch! I meka rich! I pull oppa
da guy fooma lay in godemma doidy gobitcha! Otza
shoo ting eeza got widussa. O, otza somma bum, ot
somenobitch!"

Cahoon, appalled, slapped two stiff palms on his ears,
fingers stiff, upright.

"A bloody disgrace," he whispered. "Him shaming
his immigrant parents that way. I can't take that kind
of spittin' on his mother's tongue. Bless 'em, they're
elderly folk down on Mulberry and well respected and
he sees to their support, but it's a bloody disgrace him
shaming their low birth—it's going a bit too far."

"He's quite a joker, this captain of yours," I said.

"A captain of yours now, too, Mr. Yago. Ah, well, a
shrug of the shoulders, there's nothin' else for it. By the
way, it just crossed my mind, I never did give you your
rent receipt. Here it is Wednesday night. It's layin' under
that turtletank in the kitchen. Top the mantelpiece.

Leastways that's where I saw it last. Hope little Jenny
didn't take to scribblin' on it the way she does on the
walls. Esther keeps tellin' me this wall scribblin' is a
child's natural way of spreadin' its wings. Only to
melt in the heat of life, I tell her, the heat of life. Well,
what d'you think of our landlord, Mr. Yago, now that
you met him eye to eye?"

"Oh, a complicated man."

"And I was tellin' the truth?"

"Exactly the truth."

"Whyn't you speak to him about your door?"

"And how about your five-watt bulbs?"

Ippi now drove leisurely. Judge Merchant was wiping
the windshield mist with his great linen. Cahoon quietly
searched his pockets; perhaps, after all, my rent receipt
was on his person. Discouraged, his fingers played
round his glass eye.

"A pack of lost lovers," Judge Merchant said.

"That's we, that's we," Ippi said.

"Lost ayn't the arf of it," Cahoon said. "Listen to 'em,
Mr. Yago—they sound like a bunch of guzzlin' krauts.
Middleaged scoundrels, the pair of you!"

"That's we, that's we," Ippi said. "We're in the back
stretch now, you two-buck donkeys. Otza hungry Julius
Kurl at the tape. Eeza tink e shake us down. Ho. Ho.
Hungry Yoolyus. Always pushin' the chalk horse.
Y'know—we used as kids to work together in some
lousy stall on the boardwalk. Koonyilont! Otza some
moutta-piece, ot hungry Julius. 'It's a little black bawhl,
it gizzin, it gizzout, y'givem d'whip, y'givem d'spur,
y'makem go, y'ridem jockey, it gizzin it gizzout the
little black bawhl, the winnin' tables stay lit the losers go
off, THAT'S how we very-fy the winners! A paira

nylons for the ladies, for the gents a pass to Silver's baths.' Ah, Kurl never cared how he earned his bread—he took pinches for the handbooks down on Elizabeth, a double sawbuck each. He collected the Christmas gelt from the pushcart peddlers for the precinct slushfund. Both ends to the middle. What a snake! As kids we used to call him King of the Spanish Fly. He'd sell us sugar in a capsool for the genuyine article. King of the Spanish Fly. He'd peddle old jellyroll to the chinky laundry and hot eyeglass frames to the optometrist. He'd steal a lambchop foom outta you moutt. And he looks so goshbloomed innocent, the hairy Turk!"

"Ah, well, say—" Judge Merchant said. "Bone in or bone out, the butcher doesn't lose a dime."

Church and Worth. Ippi had overshot. Down he goes. The municipal arch has a wormy coat. There was a lone lighted window in City Hall. Uptown again: Cedar, Fulton, Barclay. I felt sick, and faint. Too little food all day, too much of Ippi's mad bull. At Chambers, I asked to be let out. There, west of the corner, at the curb near a newsstand lean-to, I vomited. (Just go along, go along, Judge Merchant had said.) When I was feeling myself again, we finally reached the Thomas Street establishment of Julius Kurl.

On the first floor, a repair shop; machines alltypes. On its door hung a blue slat sign: ELECTRIFY YOUR TREADLE.

On the second floor, Kurl's place. On the landing wall at the stairhead was taped a long crinkly paper which read, under a crude black arrow: SUCKERS AND CHEWERS HALT—FLOWERS ON PREMISES! ENTRY FORBIDDEN TO APHIDS, RED SPIDERS, EXPOSED THRIPS, LEAF HOPPERS, CATERPILLARS, MEXICAN BEETLES, CLIMBING CUTWORMS!

"I guess us insects is welcome since we can't read a word, eh?" Ippi said.

"I'm a gnat and you're a fly and Cahoon's a flea and Barney's a fulltime silverfish. Prohibition to us is not explicit. Before the law we may enter," Judge Merchant said.

The florist's door had an inset of wired glass, a smoky mosaic of ordered hexagonals. On Ippi's knock a limping shadow loomed, paused, coughed, raised an arm, drew back, drew the door open.

"Well, hooray," Judge Merchant said. "If it isn't the lanky Dutchman."

"Hello, my wild little Indians," Kurl said, lanky indeed in a straw hat, toothed at the rim, chipped at the crown, and with its black ribbon shredding. "I could run a four-day fever time it takes *you* people to get anywheres. How do you like the boater?"

He looked me up and down and whistled. "And you're Mr. Barney Yago." I gave my hand and was about to speak, but something kept me still.

"You'll forgive our unpunctuality, Julius," Judge Merchant said. "It's this mad latino—you can't be sure you'll step out of his car alive."

"I'm riding with a judge, nixvar? Hell, who got the gall to write me up?" Ippi said. "Well, maybe the motorcycle boys, they can't be reached, and a couple or three a the traffic goons with a heeazard-deeazon out for the precinct. Have you ever been tagged by that tall sonofabitch of a sergeant?—that Michael Finotti? He give his own captain one the other day. He's got a hell of a rabbi, that's why. They say it's the Cardinal himself."

Hand on the doorknob, Kurl said, "I'm glad you reminded me." Out of the secret compartment of a wallet he extracted a folded green tag with a little white string on it. "Here you are, Judge, a parking violation."

"My pleasure, Julius. Though it will soon be a trifle more difficult. They're installing IBM machines to tally all the unanswereds."

"Name a machine to stand up against old Merchant," Ippi said. "On the bench a mench."

"Flattery got you everywhere," Judge Merchant said.

Kurl preceded us into a huge loft. He moved with a stiff and ugly limp.

"What's the matter with him?" I asked Cahoon.

"Who? Oh, Kurl? You refer to his limp? Why it's in your honor, Mr. Yago. He knows all about you. I mean I've been talking about you for such a hell of a long time, don't y'know. He's just puttin' it on. It's his way of makin' you feel at home. A sweet gesture, don't you think?"

"Tell him to stop that phony limp or I'll walk out of here!"

"Shh-shh-okay—though I don't see the harm in it."

"In the back room, fellows," Kurl said. "I was just about to show the girls a few slides."

We followed him through a low causeway, stooping. The floor sloped. Glistening wet, it seemed to have been recently hosed. The air, unheated, played with our mouthwarmed puffballs. Along a wallbase here and there, a chest of flowers weakly offered a kneehigh pastiche of color. We crunched over worldly litter, spike-lets and leaves, glumes and sprigs. Floral artifacts every-where. On the walls, hoisted on threepenny nails, a his-tory of previous tenancy: a French curve and T-Square, a fleecy buffer, a galvanized nipple, a fanbelt, a trucker's invoice, the belly of a Northern Muskrat skin, a paper pattern for a lady's bag, a tailor's tape, a coil of BX cable.

Near a high arched window with a low broad sill stood a cutter's table, three wide boards on a pair of wood horses, dressed with a green checkered cloth; upon it a fanciful array of cold cuts and drink. All as yet untouched. Three young women sat at the table, lighting each other's cigarettes. As we approached, they flayed at a considerable cloud, coughing a little, daintily, and laughing a little too.

"This place has the air of a Jubilee!" Judge Merchant said. "Ah, Julius, Julius. . . ."

"It's really Jeremiah," Kurl said. "Anyways, it's Julius to my intimates."

"And—ah—what is it to the ladies?" Cahoon asked.

"We'll let you know in its proper place," one girl flatly said for the three.

"The suspenders will be unbearable," Cahoon said. "How do you do, my dear? This is Barney Yago."

"How do you do?"

"How do you do? This is Mr. Cahoon."

"How do you do? This is Marge."

"How do you do? This is Judge Merchant."

"How do you do, Your Honor? This is Francie."

"How do you do? This is Mr. Ippilito."

"How do you do? This is Giselle."

"How do you do? Ah, Giselle."

"And what about me?" Kurl said. "Am I something unmentionable?"

"We'll get to you in your proper place," Judge Merchant said, winking at Giselle.

"Any you boys care for a sanitch?" Francie asked.

"Try the rollbeef it's fabliss," Giselle said. "You never tasted nothing like it even in Mr. Wolf's, I mean a filet."

"Julius—why you old *tchidrool*," Ippi said, "You remembered the guinea stinkers!"

"Well, there they are next to the pickles. I remembered you were partial to your father's kind so I sent special down to that place on Carmine your uncle runs."

"How a man can smoke them ropes is a definite question," Cahoon said.

"That shows you up for what you are, Irisher—a pink ham sandwich on white bread. You got your figgers, I got mine."

"Just a smidgin and lick of mustard," Judge Merchant said to Marge. "On that pumpernickel which makes my heart overflow. Little girl, you're too liberal with the meat."

"That tummy of yours can take it, appears to me," Marge said.

"Tummy now, in minutes a malevolent bulge," Judge Merchant said.

"Who's on the booze?" Ippi asked.

"Hep y'sef," Kurl said.

"No dear, no slaw," Cahoon said to Francie. "I can't take the soggy kind."

"It's ony a sanitch. If I wanted to serve a sponge y'd know it."

Giselle, tallest of the three, in black faille at the head of the table, kissed the tip of her ringed pinky and transferred the kiss to the tiny cleft in Francie's chin. Cahoon turned to me, his mouth full of sanitch, and whispered: "Coarse little twist, that one. By the way, Mr. Yago—ah, this little wingding—ah—I mean it's sotty voco between us men, right? I mean what Esther don't know won't hurt her. Right? I mean as far as business goes, this is a grand old American custom. Right?"

Giselle offered Cahoon some potato salad.

"No, dear—thanks just the same," Cahoon said. "I'll take no hand in ruinin' that fine parsley garden."

"Marge," Giselle said, "whyn't you show the gents those fabliss gifts we got?"

"I take care of all my little girls," Kurl said, "Just a dandy little host, that's what I am."

Out of a large handbag Marge raised three white snaplid cases. She then lowered each in line beside the platter of sliced turkey. Giselle reached forward and opened them. Incorruptible in cotton wool were two gold crosses and a Star of David.

"Who is the star meant for?" I asked.

"It's mine," said Marge.

"They're fabliss."

"We've got the makin's of the Eucharist," Cahoon said. "Now, I mean no blasphemy, Ippi. Them lovely little white boxes and all that food is what I'm referrin' to."

"The thought is what counts," Judge Merchant said.

"And a star to steer her by," Kurl said.

"Julius, you're a constant source of amazement," Judge Merchant said.

"Well, the fact is, in the diamond market uptown I've got my brother-in-law—a delicious connection. It helps."

Cahoon with whiskey refilled my paper cup. Coming close, he whispered, "You wouldn't think it now, would you? I mean that gold Star of David. I mean a fine Jewish girl out on the hustle. Very unique, I'd say."

"Many man shekels the original sin."

"Beg pard?"

Just then, Marge, chunky in a tan wool suit, deferring to Giselle's authority by turning up a palm, stood up. One hand held a paper cup, the other was on her hip.

Her face a vacancy under a harsh blond dye, she came round the table to Judge Merchant's side, and took from his pocket the flatfolded *East Side News*. She waved it, first at Cahoon, then at me, emptied her cup with a man-sized toss of her head. With a haughtiness worthy of the most heuristic of women, she faced me:

"All this gosping and whispring and you with those big baby blues. You and this pal of yours. Let's get something straight, shall we, while the party's still young? Pardon the double meaning. Yes, I'm Jewish and who could ever mistake you? I don't need you bugeyed over this *mogen-duvid* to give yourself away. *Tish, tish,* I'm laughing like a table. I'm a Marcy Avenue girl, you ever been there? Let me tell you about my clever papa who makes me so holy sentimental just thinking about him no matter what time it is. Oh he's not dead by a long shot, though it's funny I always dream of bunking into him in heaven, where he sees how really good I am and tells God. Anyways, I hope God is good to him for being so good to me. And gives him some peace of mind *aumayn*. Papa usta push raw garlic down my throat—to cure my diarreah. You know what he did for my kid brother's acne? —a compress dipped in kerosene. You know how he paid his respects to my mother, a teeny snip of a woman with bursitis? He'd fill up a thimble with milk and climb on a chair and drink her health. Let me tell you where I played doctor with my kid brother—in a stable for the horse and wagons of the Williamsburg Baking Company. And in

the celler of the *chedar* next door. Full up with
fat little roaches. You know where my father
got the kerosene for the compresses on my kid
brother's acne? —He stole it from the lamps
hanging under the horse wagons. Papa was always full of music. *Uff'n pripichik brent a
petzeleh.* You know where you could always
find him? Ed McGirr's, the corner ginmill,
playing cards with the local *shkutzim*. Can you
picture it? Papa? Cohen beef and cribbage. At
my kid brother's *bar-mitzvah,* you know what
Rabbi Meinwald said? —A Jewish father is
both a king and a prince in his own house.
Papa stood there like a king just looking at my
kid brother. My kid brother, who's going in for
teaching, calls the *bar-mitzvah* a *pipik* victory.
You know what Papa did for a living? He
owned a sweet little silver pushcart and sold
knishes. He usta wait for the kids to come out
of *cheder* and rob them gooeyed with his junky
knishes. But you never met a more *frimmeh
mench* than clever papa. You never did,
Sweetie. So here's papa's dear little girl just as
frim, only cuter, by means her precious little
precious. You know what this sweet little kooze
did for her family? Just bought them paid in
full a bunglo colony up in Highland Mills and
me a six room apartment in Tudor City with a
fulltime maid, that's all. And no questions
asked. So if you're seeling keester for Easter,
Mr. Shanda, make mine pistachio."

Returning to Judge Merchant his *East Side News,*
Marge walked to the high, arched window and joined

her two friends; the three looked in silence into the quiet street. I followed, to ask her to join me in a sandwich and drink, and to explain that neither I nor my friends were moral kings involved in special intrigue, but were there, simply, for enjoyment, which she was profession-bound to see to, her clever papa being no business of mine.

(How would she handle my stump? . . . As she finds it? She, herself, was far from perfection. Conjuring trouble, I am doomed to walk backward the rest of my life.)

Marge, too, the flatvoiced whore, had her head turned round conjuring clever papa. Her tresses fell back over coppernosed breasts. (I wondered, does she weep? Then her tears run down to track her sweet young buttocks. *Pulkies,* she'd call them. The hindmost of sorrow, a rump to lay my stump on. Sweet, young rump, trumpet not thy conquest! . . . *jumpfer nit!*)

"Damn touchy, that twist," Cahoon said, coming close behind me. "Tilly Williams herself—she's odd and queer, but she ayn't arf peculiar. Don't waste your pity."

At the window, Giselle said something to Marge which I could not hear.

"Oh, Selly," Marge answered, "Don't be an old craphat."

The lights went out.

"Oh, come on, you depressing bandits," Kurl said. "I thought this was a party! Now everybody find a seat and I'll show the slides. I want you to see what you're paying for!"

Groping and grabbing, with much colliding and excuse-mes, I found a seat flanked by Ippi and Giselle, facing the projection screen. Marge began a skillful wiping of Judge Merchant's sticky fingers with his own linen. Then, she tested her effort with kisses. Cahoon, with Francie, hid behind a column of round corrugated boxes. Kurl fussed at the slide machine.

"When a man's in love the whole world looks knock-kneed," Cahoon said, "Even in the dark."

"Hey, don't you never cut your fingernails?" Francie asked.

"Ah, my dear," Cahoon replied, "I see it's raining again."

Ippi leaned close, said into my ear: "That janitor'll go out talkin', so help me."

"But it's a wilder rain than previous," Cahoon said, still unseen, for the benefit of all. "Much wilder."

I turned to the high window, saw the rain falling, lit up by a neon across the way.

"By the time any rain gets down to us in this city it's a shameful muddy stew, now, isn't it?" Cahoon said. "The Good Lord wringin' out his mop all over his dirty floor."

"Who knows better than a maintenance engineer?" Ippi called out to him, over my head.

"But it's a full rain fallin' fast on this winter's night," Cahoon said, pretending indifference. "Though winter has no special claim to it, now, does it?" (Such a rain falls in summer as well as autumn, y'll agree? Down she comes full and fuzzy on every part of the big town, on old Trinity and St. Pat's, on the Exchange, Columbia, the Custom House, on the old museums, on the rollin' boulders in the Park, on the flatbottoms up of the row-boats, on the ballparks and ferryboats, on North Brother Isle and the Navy Yard, on the, let's see, one—two—three—four—five great bridges, on the Wallabout front, the Tombs, on all the channels, basins, and water hooks,

the slips and bays, on the perfect streets and mutinous
children, on Kings County herself, down she comes
bleary and greasy, on the roof over our own poor heads,
on the peddler carts on Avenue C, on buildings no one
cares to notice, on the dear East River too, only to be
swallowed up and swum out to the sea with the sewer-
ins. Now where in the name of Jesus doesn't she fall?)

Giselle had a head cold. When the lights were on, were
her red eyes ugly? Her colds, she explained, were
leeches, bloating on her strength, though she smeared
herself with mustards and rubs, down to the hidden
seas where men sail to fish and grapple. While Kurl
fussed at the slide machine, and while Giselle unbut-
toned me, she lamented her glaucous phlegm and hack-
ing. This tall whore foresaw her own untimely death.
(A younger brother, Peanuts, dead at twelve, went
caulking the city's cracks and seams with rainbow colored mucus. Our city treads on spittoon cobbles, its
pulse a throbbing respirator.)

By matchlight, there was a new flurry of movement
round the food table, more passing and capsizing of
paper plates and cups, a whistling jeer directed at the
projectionist, his apology, his reminder, to the men, that
we were squandering our cover of darkness. A debate
rose up on where to put the plates and cups. Francie appeared from behind the corrugated column. While
Cahoon lit her way with matches; she collected and
cleared the troublesome things. Her escort then led her
back behind the column.

"Julius," Judge Merchant said, "maybe we can see
those slides another time."

"I've come this far without a hitch; hold your water."

"Good for you, little Potpie," Giselle said.

"So *that's* what the ladies call you!" Cahoon said, loud and clear, from behind his column. "Sometimes we call him Sip the Dip," Giselle said.

"Oh, yes—Sip the Dip," Marge said.

"You'll get to see why later on," Giselle said, softly, into my ear. "He's reserved his favorite steambath down on Suffolk from three o'clock on. I just hope you're thirsty enough!"

Of his thumb and index Kurl made a hornpiece and gave a low kazoolike toot. "Roll 'em!"

Sssssss-LICK. A flue of light. Sssssss-LICK. A picture.

"Hey, what's that?" Marge said.

"Sorry, wrong slide."

"What is it, Julius?"

"The stamen and pistil of a sweetpea."

"The stamen and whatil?"

"Pistil." Kurl fussed again. "These I borrowed from a friend with the Board of Education. Teaches biology. Now wait, I'll get them all in order."

Sssssss-LICK. "Oh, damn!"

"What's that one?" Giselle said.

"That? —Now, let's see—now that would be the anther lobes of a pansy. Now hold on a minute, hold the flow, folks, oh, mercy, ah, here we go!"

Sssssss-LICK. A flower.

"Ooooooo!"

At sight of Kurl's first item on the screen, Ippi leaned across Giselle (testing the heft of her bosom) and put a pad and pencil in my lap.

"Take notes," he said. "You can't sell people on something you're ignorant. Then we'll make a graph of the weekly collections. It's professional. Take notes."

.   .   .

So, there in the dark, by fits and starts, in force a babble of eight, the lecture. Kurl, the cozy botanist, exhibited bearded Iris, with petals fall and standard, three each. He, exuberant, blessed for devotion the hardy perennial. To blossom under cruelest neglect! As each flower appeared, he tipped his straw hat. Laughed with love. His competence held us fixed; that of the three girls too. Fingerwise. Catch at basal whiskers. Iridescent. *"Not for tickling, smartie!"* Stalkborne, the billygoat! With type genus family specie the man was most charitable. Can't be beat for accent, even in a dismal ditch. Character? Why, he ventured, the swollen rootstock. Synthetic and loam, three perfumes. Orchard-like. Fagsmoke winding in the lightflue. By which I made my notes. Soft rot the chiefest trouble. Really good in front of shrub! Approach is all! *"Damn your fingernails, Mr. Cahoon!"* I wish bearded Iris spread throughout city. Munificent! Why not? Coenties Slip to Baker Field! Lightly flushed in lemon. Nine to twelve buds in succession of bloom. A darling plant, no? (Prodded by Ippi, Giselle plunged, and between my thighs her bracelets rang.) Rhizome! *"Why so gloomy, honey?"* (My industrious hand to her hidden sea. Different at night, I know!) Lavender-blue. From the haft to the falls those tufty beards. Sssssss-LICK. The Cockscomb! Stiff, formal, good for bedding. *"Honey, you do have your heart set on Marge!"* Red yellow pink rose. I detest the spiky cluster! Annual. (Giselle put my hand on her pitchy hair.) Winter's bouquet, a marvel. Oh, for a vial of it! (Francie squealed, your tigernail!) Needs a textured soil. Celosia. Bright sun. (Is it because she's Jewish?) Watch the red spider! Bushy the plant, the crested plume. Can you see the shoreline sown? Or, Chelsea, say? Warm sun. *"Why do you hope I'm thirsty?"* Pa-

tience! Popular pot. Sssssss-LICK. The Foxglove! *"I'm
Jewish too, one-eighth!"* First herbaceous. *"My mother's a northern spik, pop's a pimp. The old lady'd have
me under a king! Do you believe that acne and that
kerosene?"* Not too showy. Self-perpetuity. A plant of
dignity, a leaf of poison. Imagine! Medicinal? Diuretic!
*"D'you know Francis Wellerky? Honey, I'll take a beer
any old time! The girl is simply father-locked!"* Thim-
ble-shaped flower, purple yellow white. A pest is a pest.
Nutty red! Juices are sucked from the underside. Digi-
talis! I've hybridized freely in Mount Morris Park.
(Hear the Judge, laughing like a kid!) Expect a whitish
injury. (At her own pleasure she sniffs the wind. So
superior. If it's deep, it's Jewish! I know!) Spires are
foils for other forms. (Gentile teeth bite a Jewish breast!
Now, isn't that a disgrace?) Sssssss-LICK. The Gas-
plant! *"Lord, I'm high! Honey, can't I make you forget her?"* Handsome, sturdy, three feet high. Fraxinella,
if you like! Dittany. *"This I love, hard as a rock."* Will
outlast even the Peony. Interval stagger, best effect. I
see the whole of Chinatown! Dictamnus. (Ippi's here
with his hoghorn. Crafty wop!) Leathery and ash-like.
Lemony scent. Delicious! *"Come close: Kurl is freakish!
Have you ever seen his dildo box?"* Fall seeding, spring
up. Might sulk before contentment! (Positively human!) Sssssss-LICK. The Monkshood! *"Did you ever?"*
Picture with a big white mum! *"You're my very first
bookwriter! Write me a poem, a wild one."* Wolfsbane!
Blue, violet, sometimes white. Tuberous roots. So
deadly! *"I could learn to love you, Honey!"* Don't you
adore the long raceme? Pretty up Church Street in
showy hood. The Cyclamen mite is your real affliction.
*"Oh, you thing, you kiss me while you think of Marge!
Lord, I'm glad that Ippi's gone. You're too late, lover,*

she's spoken for. Please." Ovotran. Don't take it for an edible! *Say, ain't the janitor and Francie playing it dumb?* Foliage twin: Delphinium. Where is that guinea spit of earth? The pedicel tells, disturb ye not the unders! *"Yes, I hate her damn superior puss! See both of us naked, then decide!"* Poor germination, why do I show it? *"Look me in the face, you sonofabitch!"* Ssss-sss-LICK. Snapdragon! Now a strain resistant to rust. *"What's wrong with me?"* Crown risen spikes go five feet. Stake the taller kind. *"It's lonely! You'd think on her mattress even death would come!"* They flower spectacular the second year. Prefer an alkaline. *"Her mouth is wet, big boy, she knows the way! Why do I lower myself?"* Sow in August, the young move into a cold-frame. *"Write me a poem. A wild one! A dark one!"* Wide in color. Majus! Pinch for branching. *"Isn't there one little thing about me? My sinner's legs? Old uglyfang you!"* Coppery-red, a scarlet clear. Mulch; caution. I'll tell you where, in Stuyvesant town! Observe the blight, the anthracnose. In man a boil malignant! *"So I'm not Jewish. So I'm not the stars in heaven. But I can hush you in my arms."* Split the seam and see the sap tube! Black! *"Honey, I'm not all bad."* Sssssss-LICK. The Dwarf-phlox! Excel up front, shines the rock. *"How do you like it?"* Girls, are you earning your keep? Andicola. A lovely garden spread. The mat is dense! Needle leaf. Can you see the alpine lawn? Take Division Street. *"Lost? Loose? What? Your pelvic harness?"* Each is a slender thing! Cluster-borne! Solitary! *"How the night? Lonely! Even in the sand. Lonely!"* Never mind the dead-looking brown. *"Marge is a belly-wrench."* You're content with simply magenta? *"Oh, I've got you now!"* Sphagnum-moss on the seed bed. Rocky high! *"You like me just a little?"* Sssssss-LICK.

Scabiosa! My, such a party! Anybody left who cares?
Mourning-bride. White through cream through blue.
Through blue. Some are rank, untidy. Average thrive.
"Cahoon's a puppypad now, hear? Awful quiet. Dear-
heart, it's an evening's work. Night for us is the after-
life!" Sweet scabious! Soft. Gray. No pincushion this,
lacy. Collar of leaves. What's a name? Weedy too. Even
a sill on Henry Street. It's haunting. *"She flaunts it."*
Variety Webbiana. *"Would you want me sly and lip-*
less? Like her?" Sssssss-LICK. Why, h'llo m'dam
Kniphofia! There are them to whom it's Torch-lily.
Or Poker-plant. Grisly! Full sun a soil well drained.
"All right, you nosy boy: Marge dips her breast in a
bowl of punch! Kurl's game." Soft red, orangered. No
need the nicotine spray. *"The bowl is passed, you drink!*
Think of it. You drink of it. Sip the Dip, you see?"
Tritoma! Quite showy on the border. Team to the Edel-
weiss for Yorkville folk. Wooly-white, that one. Yours
the choice. Seventy species known to man. The old
leaves stay! Till spring! *"Giselle my name—I'll who're*
you in a minute! Dry your tears! She's gone! Your
mine! No switch. She's down!" White-fairy! Crown-of-
gold! Coral-sea! Vanilla! Sssssss-LICK. Cosmos! End
of shoot! Crimson to white, yellow to orange. Deep
cut; feathery leaf. Sparse and leggy, needs the stake!
"Now you're talking! No angels we, sweet hoteye."
Choose your fiend, it's all the same. Where's your god-
dess? Quenched? Easy come! Sulphureous! All over
the town, any old place. Buttermilk Channel to Inwood
Hill. *"Lord, Lord, buckets and lakes! Out! Oh!"* True-
asblue? *"What did you say?"*

The lights went on. Ippi was at the switch, having
watched the latter flowers from there. Kurl was at his

slide machine. Francie appeared from behind the corrugated column. She approached the banquet table, appraised it, walked slowly round it. Cahoon followed,
but remained apart. The Judge rose with effort, Marge
behind him. Spent, I reviewed without interest my lecture notes. Giselle, returned by puff and primp to the
full measure of her poise, joined the sluggish walk
round the table. Marge revived her strut: her coldness a
high panache. They served one another Benedictine,
which they sipped weakly. We men now entered upon
an aftermatch of grace and quietude.

But while they walked round the table, the girls made
ready to leave. It was two A.M. Not a word had been
uttered. They were fully repainted. A button had
snapped off one of Judge Merchant's tweed spats; in
search of it he combed the floor with his *East Side News*.
However, he soon gave this up. Ippi walked to Kurl
at the slide machine.

"It's too late now, you fool," Ippi said.

"Oh, let's give it a try," Kurl said.

"Enough is enough, Julius."

"Just one, please, only one."

"Only one, then we'll get out of here."

Sssssss-LICK. A slide. All turned to the screen again.
Upon it, weakly, in the fagsmoke mist, in the overhead
lights, two naked women lay in a heap of pillows on
a leopard rug. One held a whip of leopard tails, the other
a tasseled drapecord. Kurl laughed and began to shake
the slide machine. The picture trembled. Unsealed, the
women swelled. Red nails scratched the screen. Pillows
sagged under the weight of flesh. Hands kneaded thighs
in a drifting of limbs, and, upon Kurl's mischief, a full
breast jelled. Malignant mouths laughed back at him.

"Whoopee!"

"Julius, will you ever grow up?" Giselle said.

"Dear old Sip and his family album," Marge said.

"Just you sip your brandy, girl, and shut up," Kurl said.

He pulled the slide out of its slot, switched off the projector.

"Are we off to Suffolk Street, or aren't we?" Giselle said.

"We're going. My, we're all so bored. My first little picture in plain talk and we all come down with eye-strain. Well, would you like me to be a merry Andrew and put a match to it? Goodness, a little salt on the bawdry won't hurt nobody never! Go arrest me. Powder my socket and kiss my sinew. Aren't we the sanctimonious little cousins club! So now I'm the stinker, I'm the brute. It's a wonder we can sip our brandy, we're all so goddam pure. It makes me spit! Oh, come on—lets go take ourselves a cold plunge."

We filed out of the warehouse. Behind me, Cahoon said: "You'll have to parn his moods, Mr. Yago; now, what would you venture to call this one? The spit Kurl?"

Three to the front, five to the rear, Ippi's car, pounding its shaft, turned left into West Broadway, grinding and rocking, and left again on Duane. Cahoon, beside me, remarked on the return of the dirty mist. Francie was bundled in his lap. His arms were coiled round her waist, his fingers quibbled in secret on her secret points. On their right, the Judge, with Marge in his lap, pumped and wheezed, while he remarked his preference for the wilder rain. In front, Giselle and Kurl tried to quell Ippi's extravagance at the wheel. The lap girls asked for smokes, and the Judge, his hands the agents of his grace, managed, out of an oppressed lowland, to pluck two cigarettes.

"Mind your ashes," he said.

"Well, what'll we do with them?" Marge said.

"There's an old tin can up near the window behind you," Ippi called back.

"An old tin can is for any gentleman what deserves it," Marge said.

The ashes fell. Soon, it seemed, nothing but ash-frost remained of us.

"That last slide was a nasty piece of business," Cahoon whispered to me. "No need to pull a stunt like that! Francie, dear, I can't hold you up much longer!"

"Listen to the man," Francie said. "You'd think his knees were creampuffs!"

"Now, Mr. Cahoon," Kurl said, "this is a hellish time to peter out! You've a whole night before you!"

"Lead on," Cahoon said.

This ride raged bitterer than the first. Ippi was incensed by our admonitions and made us dizzy with his turns and stops.

"Must you keep on bumping me?" Marge said to Francie.

"Say listen, honey," Francie said, "when are you going to quit using those bacon strips to lubricate your skin?"

Marge turned to Cahoon: "They tell me your basement accommodations go for a quarter a night. What are your weekend rates?"

"It's a dirty vicious lie!"

"It had better be," Judge Merchant said. "It had better be."

"Here we are!" Kurl said. "Suffolk Street might be under skunk cabbage now, but just you wait. Oh what

won't we never do to it? Sunny cowslips and pussy wil-
lows and sprackly jack-in-the-pulpits. We'll dance on a
carpet of yellow pollen. Just picture us walking up
those squeaky old steps with jonquils and harebells to
sweeten our heels!"

Kurl, the visionary, opened the door, stepped lightly
into his mind's meadow. Giselle followed. She said:
"Watch your step, everybody—the hounds are loose!"

"Looks like Arab's work," Cahoon said. "He's been
known to wander this far south."

"Bark hazard!" the Judge said.

"Barooof!" Ippi said.

Narrow stoopsteps. Narrow door, not fit to turn
round in. Over it, a rusted tin sign: NEW YORK BATH-
HOUSE. Under this, another: SUFFOLK STREET BLOCK AS-
SOCIATION—A PEOPLE UNITED BY A PURPOSE. Raising her
plangent arm to it, Giselle said: "Sure, money."

On our left, Sig Fingergold Mausoleums. (Sandblast
the face, braze the inscription. Our loved ones shall
suffer no seepage.)

The hall beyond the stoop was too dark to see
through, so we formed a chain, hand-in-hand, with
Kurl leading us to the rear. He called our attention to a
waisthigh guide rope, which ran, from spike to spike,
along the lefthand wall. Its touch made the blood run
cold. Slimed and pulpy, a ruminant's bowel.

"Oh, Jesus!" I yelled. "What a way to end the night!
Bibber, old man, where are you? With our own *vomp'n*
we shall hang ourselves! *Shalom shalom v'en shalom!*"

Kurl instructed us all to wait, and faded into an il-
lusion of a low proscenium arch. But a door, which we
could not see, closed, with a swine-wet thud. Behind it
was a yet darker space, for, when it had been open, not
a single thing was seen.

"What's this all about?" I asked Cahoon.

"He's checking. Just checking. Old Leibush who runs this place—y'know, the old man who lives top of Bibber in our building—well, Leibush is a bit irresponsible. He finds it hard to honor a reservation. Kurl gives him his price and then some to have the place all to ourselves, but Leibush can't look a seethin' pot in the eye without bein' a prophet unto *all* the nations. Once you get my meanin'. He's got the mental outlook of a public utility; there's not enough money in all the world to suit him. He don't turn nobody down. He'll sneak in what he can, though the place is ours by rights. It gets a bit sticky —I mean, what with strangers gallavantin' round in a private party."

"He's a petty thief, is that what you're trying to say?"

"Oh, I *like* the man! It's ony he's got a proper nose for smellin' out our weakpoints. I mean, you just don't go bringin' oh, say, girls, into a public bath; I mean, bathe them in the same place at the same time as you. It's a common practice, all right, I agree, all over this blessed city. But there are legalities. Now Leibush, who knows this to be a business arrangement, turns a deaf ear and a blind eye to the problem. And what with His Honor present, the old goat can bargain off his greedy ways."

"And Kurl keeps coming back for more?"

"It's the man's sense of loyalty. He's a terrific old bird, that Kurl."

"Yes. Vulture-sweet."

"That's a bit strong, son."

"The company I keep is nothing short of memorable."

"You'll parn my frankness, Mr. Yago, but your stuffed-shirt opinions are about as much use round here as tits on a boar-hog."

Again, the swine-wet thud. Kurl was back. For a moment, there in this depth of darkness, with reminiscent smells of my own hall boiling off the walls, there was no talk. We paused in weariness. "Thank God I'm an atheist," Kurl said, "I can't really blame Providence or anything else for this embarrassing situation. I can only blame my own stupidity. Imagine trusting that little bag of tricks. Five hundred times and I haven't learned yet. D'you know he's got *people* sloshing round in there? And I reserved this place over a week ago! I'm furious. Listen, I could waltz us all into a bowling alley and get more satisfaction; I mean, for all the privacy we'll get that I paid him damned good money for! Oh, we'll get in, don't you worry. That fat little skunk isn't going to kill off the night just like that. Why do I keep beating my wings and come back here all the time? Him and his colonic irrigations. He knows what he can do with them! Oh, it's his damned arrogance! And for what? No Turkish, no pine, no Swedish, no gym, no solarium, no massage, no sulphur, no mud, no whirlpool, no salts, no sunlamp—a pool the size of a teapot and a steamroom with about as much *scald* as a piece of old toast. Him and his fat little ladies and their dirty little whatever they are—*mikvahs?* He thinks the perfumes of Araby float out of his walls. The horrid little bum. Come on—let's go in!"

The yet darker space beyond the door was merely a vestibule between the hall and the steambath proper, bare except for a leaftable and lamp. As we filed through, Kurl turned on the lamp, which cast a baleful light. In the corner behind it a floormop stood inverted, stiff and stringy, its locks fallen over the globular shade. The vestibule walls were tiled and sweating; wet silt covered the cement floor. Marge, comb in hand, went to the mop. Tenderly, she put the comb through its grizzly tresses. "It'll never wave, honey," she said to it quite flatly. "I know what you're suffering. Pat pat pat. Nope. Oh, sister, look at the dandruff! When's your birthday, I'll send you a waveset. Febyerry twenty-first? Hey, that's mine too! Isn't it warm in here with all these clothes on? But we girls got to stick together, no? But you're dead now, little sister, aren't you? You and that hairdo. But I remember you, little moppet, even with all these bad people round in this bad place and I remember how we lived together, even though you slept in the pantry hanging on a hook and I had a human being's bed. Remember how you loved me, you were my best friend? You remember what a happy family we were? Sleep soft in your grave, little ropyhead, I'll never forget you. I'll always be grateful. No matter how many times I drowned you or made you filthy you were nothing else but kindness personified. God bless you forever, little sister moppet, and may you rest in peace on God's floor in heaven. *Aumayn*."

"Chatty little twist, that one," Cahoon said as we squared the pool to the locker-room, a paltry enclosure of board and beam, beyond which the steamroom waited. A smell of the beach was in the air, of urinal troughs, of lettuce leaves. Two old men walked by us, indifferent to the presence of our women.

"Ah—you see what I mean?" Kurl said.

The two were bound in coils of linen, and they slapped barefoot over the wet floor, shrunken and hunched within their garments, which were twisted, and drawn out front between their thighs. Their hands held tight the flapping excess of cloth. They had come from the steamroom, pink and spongy, not minding the residual silt underfoot, from which we, with our shoes on, shivered and grimaced. Though their indifference to us was willful, they were clearly in trouble. They dared not free the cloth, for the bathhouse could not hide their nakedness. Their four interchangeable feet were clotted with nodes and purple warts in a risen tangle of veincords. Each foot was heel-gross, ankle-jagged and boiled white, the skin corrugated, every glistening toe hatted by a corn in a ring of hair.

"There, Mr. Yago," Cahoon said, "you have the glorious feet of a pair of ancient waiters. Henick and Winograd, two great pals of your old pal Bibber, now retired and livin' on their monthly checks, may the good Lord bless the Congress. I'll wager old Bibber is slappin' round here someplace. Tell me, have you ever seen feet to resemble those? Old Henick t'boot was a barber once, a partner to Kipler next door our building, and they fell out when Kipler embarked on his little numbers game. Just look at them feet! The whole neighborhood loves them two, did y'know that? Specially Winograd, with his highblood pressure and his constipation. Imagine the miles they trudged, from far-off kitchens to the borders of the wild and starving. Ah, they grew old in grace, them two, Mr. Yago, and every blessed slave that genuflected under their trays gave tribute! They'll go together, mark my words! And then, son, you'll see a heavenly sight—a thousand waiters carryin' the regal biers down to Cuylers Slip; there we'll set the remains on one of them McAllister tubs, or one that hauls the sugar coastwise into harbor and sound. The tub'll be all white in sugar-frost. They'll be laid out hard by the deck-winch, and we'll pile round their caskets all their warrior's gear: two great carvin' knives stabbed like swords into the coffins; kitchenware piled up high; on each breast a monkey-dish gilded with a coat of arms; and a spoon in each cold fist to speak of their calling. We'll set the tub to drift, out, out, mournful and sad between Governor's Isle and Ellis, and out beyond the ferry ways into Great Upper Bay, and there we'll lose sight of 'em, these kingly two on the royal barge, launched by foe and friend alike."

And still indifferent, the two old men sat at a porcelain-top kitchen table near the edge of the pool. The girls, meanwhile, had passed into the locker room, to change into bathhouse linens. Henick and Winograd engaged a deck of cards. Suddenly Winograd bent in pain over the table.

Fully clothed, we went to the table to assist.

"If you're sick, you belong home in bed," Kurl said.

"My friend," Henick said, "lie down with a dog you'll stand up with lice. For twelve years I warned this man not to walk into *shvitz* like a stuffed elephant. No! Here you have a person who eats looking over his shoulder, any minute the knuckles of a new pogrom knocking on his door. A good year for wine, a bad year for cheese, it doesn't matter, it doesn't matter to him what's on the table, it's all sucked up into Winograd's mouth. My two-legged vacuum cleaner. Then of course he runs to *shvitz*. Out of his kitchen onto the street. Out of the street into the steam. Out of the steam into the cold pool. It's in his belly the pogrom is, two and a half yards *knubblevusht*. Nine ninety-nine, the old man with the beard. Go start a game of pinochle with him. D'you know what he'll meld? A flush in cramps!"

"Is there anything we can do?" Judge Merchant asked.

"No. He'll be over it in a minute."

There was a shriek just then from the locker room, and Ippi hurried off to investigate. He returned to us to say that our three women, while winding each other into sheets, had seen a cat voyage by with a chickenwing in its mouth.

"Hooray!" Henick said. "Hooray, the war is over! Leibush's cat, that old broken-down cat, can you believe it? At last he coaxed a little food out of Leibush! The man was ready to close up, he hated the cat so much. For years he's been starving the poor kitty to get rid of it. Ah! So now Leibush threw him something. Well, I tell you. Imagine! That old wreck of a cat! So underneath it all there's a regular heart beating. Maybe he's put aside the whole chicken for his cat?"

"The girls only seen the chickenwing," Ippi said. "We need the corpus delicti to toast the cat's victory. Right, Judge?"

"The wing of a fowl in the mouth of a cat while not, I agree, the aggregate of ingredients required to establish the fact in breach of the law, or, in this instance, while not as conclusive as, say, the head, which, prima facie, would establish the slaughter, it can, this wing, in light of our experience with all specie of fowl, be taken as final proof of the mortal wound. Why if the fowl in substance is not now in the possession of Leibush, it must have hopped off somewhere to join its father in the pure domain."

"Lets hope that the old cock doesn't come back to haunt us on behalf of its child," Cahoon said.

"It's happened before," Kurl said.

"Where?" Ippi said. "Bay Ridge?"

We left them to wait our turn for the locker room. Winograd issued a weak sigh. Judge Merchant kept looking back at the two old men. After heaping his coat and jacket on a chair, he pulled and snapped his sleeve garters, pumped the Tamemand ring up and down on his finger, twittered his polygonal pendant along its platinum chain. (Had these two old men recognized him? Tweed spats, the dead give-away!) He moved quickly behind us. He began to fret first one shoe, then the other, on its opposite pantleg, as if, by force of rubbing, he might graft each spat onto the striped cloth, graft away his shoes, his legs, his entire flesh, his mortality, to become a ghost in this steaming hall. (Word of mouth would ruin him; these neighborhood wags were deadly.)

Kurl stood stooped and squareheaded against the locker-room door. His melancholy over the presence of outsiders would not be purged away. The Judge suggested to him that we hurry out of that place. There was a muted council. His Honor was assured by Cahoon that the waiters, whom the janitor knew, were ignorant entirely of His Honor's identity, of Ippi's, of Kurl's, of mine. His Honor would not be calmed. (Rather whistle now than whine later. There is much to be watchful for.)

To each of us the Judge turned. He reckoned our accounts, our personal stakes: the cold dross of scandal would make our futures worthless. (Trust in his wisdom.)

To me, his youngest, newest associate, he gave an uncle's counsel. For this night at least hadn't I had enough of revel? Morning is near, we all look a bit pale. Tomorrow there is serious work to be done. Why tax a whore's wit? As a host, the lanky Dutchman had thus far delivered himself sublimely of his obligations. Would I agree?

I explained to the Judge that I had no objections. In my own dear kitchen tub my flesh finds its own sweet peace.

Ah, commendable, advisable, the Judge remarked. (As the glow quits the glow-worm we must retreat from public pools.)

Ippi did not agree. He disdained to see the Judge wilt; the weight of clothes, not fear of public reprisal, had muddled our brains. After all, it was Ippilito who had stepped aside during Kurl's lecture and sacrificed his his portion of love, so that I, the Judge's newfound ward, might have the full measure of Giselle's attentions. (Henick and Winograd were not sea-monsters, there were no squids to ink the pool-bed, the pool was smooth and no heaving sea, without surge to tempt our labors; no man-eaters, no pig-toes beached by storm, nothing bloated, nothing dead. Why be cautious? The girls were ours till morning's light; not often is a man so opportuned by playmates. Ippi had as much to fear by exposure as any man; his Captaincy, his investments real and spiritual, promotions tried and true. He held full reign over our neighborhood merchants. Ten fingers in twice as many pies; notions, bobbins, household aids, credit and faith were his sceptre and crown; decency, the golden rule. This bounteous world of gift and stock! After all, the impulse to manly truth is not self-denial.

Well, the Judge replied, you must submit, there are no fixed vows.

Kurl concurred in Ippi's view. There is among five thieves precious little honor if we can fly against our natures.

"What do you mean *thieves?*" Cahoon said.

"Oh, be still!" Kurl said.

The florist, too, though gloomy, saw no reason to pay the trollop for work unfinished and send her peevish and sullen into her next turn. Her heart would vulgarize the kindness. What sort of man would clench a fist to

mock a fig? Ippi knew all about this! Kurl would not
abide the gesture. These three girls—why, their final
uses we haven't even begun to explore! It is simply a
matter of business. Quit now, you underwrite Leibush
and his cheating. Stay, perhaps you force his hand for
future nights. The guilt is his, not ours. We would
never forgive ourselves!

Leibush appeared, pushing a rickety service cart. On
his way by he deferred to me briefly. I wondered if he
knew the Judge to be our landlord. He was not the "fat
little skunk" that Kurl had called him, but as tall as Cahoon, though heavier, wrinkled, puffed and bagged. His
years had passed dank and humid, with towels round
his neck, in sweatshirts, ducks, and beachshoes. He
moved by a process of saturation. Another drop ab-
sorbed would start him trickling. He stepped sodden
over an imaginary pulp, his face poachy, his eyes lachry-
mose, envisioning an eternity without a single pair of
hands to wring him out!

Pushing his rickety cart to Henick and Winograd, he
gave a whistle, became a little jiggish, and made the most
of the irony of waiting on waiters. He motioned to us,
inviting our participation. A bottle of whiskey, an array
of smoked fish—(Would we rather wait for the girls to
come out?) His solicitations pendulated between us and
the two old men, and he slithered round the table and
cart, pouring drinks, talking, singing, whistling, display-
ing food. Like ivy round a tree he twined himself round
his arguments: Ah—why shouldn't we unbend? Why
persevere in petty claims? He could not with conscience
throw these two old men out into the street. In bathhouse sheets who can tell which paunch is privileged,
which is not? From crotch to gorge we are all the same,
candles melting as one. The steamroom will see to our

transformations, painlessly. But it is essential to shed our
street clothes! (Come, come, try a slice *kopchunka;* delicious. Color of mother of pearl. Plate carp? Sturgeon?
Not lake, *beluga.* Crinkly sprats, golden chubs; spawn
of sociability. Black *m'slinnes?* A *fligg'l? Shpitz* of pumpernickel? An anchovy? Snip of kipper? The onion's
fried, the herring's baked. Salt to make us drink to make
us sweat to make us clean. *Matjes mahreneerta?* History
of *miltz* and craft. Rollmop? *R'uslich?* Some bloater?
Try the Bismarck; two bearded dwarfs toting their own
hindquarters. Pickles?—home-made, in a cool, dark cellar, pressed heavy in the barrel, on the bushel-lid a
smooth brown rock awash in brine and bayleaf.)

Tucked and pinned in secret places, the girls came out
of the locker room. Bathhouse linens were passable
gowns. The fluorescent tubes overhead cast a pale pearly
gray through the room, and our women came toward
us as if through a scrim. Perspiring, the girls possessed
a certain cunning and mystery. They carried their hand-
bags away from themselves at forearm's length, steering
them through the muggy air. An involuntary noise came
out of Leibush's throat. Consummation was at hand!
He dragged a wooden schoolyard bench between the
cart and table. After drying it off a bit with the ends of
their cloths, the girls sat, and waited to be told what
course to follow.
Giselle poured drinks for herself and the others. I had
asked her before why it was she who commanded. Well,
. . . she had found them in an Eighth Avenue bar,
amateurish, in their dime rags uninviting even to a Sunday soldier. They were, however, willing, with an ambition for money touching in its purity. (A woman's
body must be the minister of her ambition, schooled in

all diplomacies to bend softly, like a flower, to every horror that men will bring her. Her heart must remain ster-
ile to their sentiments, unpolluted by their secrets; she
must hide her hate beneath her lace, and hum to herself
of money, for money is the fruitful river, the pain in the
dream which wakens us all. There is but one revision to
a willing girl's style: puberty.)

Giselle was a Ridgewood girl. On a gray stoop,
under dead windows, she had learned to snap
her fingers. Onderdonk and Himrod, dead and
gray, a rain-gray corner, woodburnt dusks,
smoky winters, charflakes for her Christmas
snow. Peanuts died of leukemia. Papa arranging
customers for Mama, the Castilian lady on the
Heiny street. (My Catholic kings.) Not a Jew in
ten square blocks. Driven out: unity in Ridgewood, pure in race. Her kitchen floor the Apos-
tolic See, a daily procession to the number of
twelve. On the kitchen floor men rolled where
Mama's vapors floated. As they came out, dry-
lipped and pale, she snapped her fingers in their
teeth. They pinched her cheek: little girl, you're
cute. They gave her a penny. Where's that smile,
honey? Give us a smile, come on. (Mama
called me her mother-in-law. Papa said I belonged in an institution, my attachment to that
stoop was unnatural. He gave me a nickel for
an O'Henry bar. Mama saved her plate and silver; so a dowry grows. Nickels and pennies:
my profitable stoop.) On the low gray stoop
she supped on Mama's stew, haslets, hearts,
honey? Give us a smile, come on. (Mama
lies with Peanuts now, in Mt. Judah near the

reservoir. Her vapors coil round her baby's
bones, enchant voracious worms. On Cypress
and Decatur, Papa lives with a Berlin beauty,
their terrace the top of a movie marquee.
Changeless Ridgewood, changeless streets, ritual of dead windows, burning wood, Palmetto,
Woodbine, Woodward, Grove: names of nature.
In Grover Cleveland Park my innocence lies,
gazing up, winking at passing wings. A sod of
memory, planted there by a boy from Weirfield
Street. (He taught me to smoke.)

But Francie, Francie is a Throg's Neck girl.
On reefs and sandbars, yacht-club boys came
maundering. (Say, what is a Throg anyways?)
Francie will sail with you, long as there's *gelt*
astern. Seeds of cunning, troll and tease, grains
of sand in the cleft of her breasts. The hottest
trick is dealt on dunes, nipples hard to the cool
salt air. Why, the girl's a water-nymph! A clean
east wind blowing dead west. And the girl to
bail you out! Girls get round, why the look?
(So what's a Throg?) There's a Throgmorton
Street in London, one off Eastchester Bay.
Francie doesn't care how young you are, your
money is old enough. Her folks are up there
still, on Pennyfield Avenue, ain't that pretty?
Her father's a retired fireman, sweet as they
come, a wonderful man; he'd tip his hat to you
for giving his engine the right of way. But her
mother walks the beaches blowing bubble gum,
a woman in her fifties, telling strangers she's
pregnant t.d.m.m. Francie's been spooned out
twice by an Armenian midwife, a fat old cow,
two C notes a scrape; on her purple beret she

wears a gold lieutenant's bar. Francie was married once, to a cardboard collector (a musician
gone bad). He roams the city behind a wagon,
a razor in his teeth. Oh, she was taught her arith-
metic in Ferry Point Park, by writing in the
sand. Clean wind, trick-studded sea, positions
marked in the azure dawn, so calm, so clear.

"I'll bet that pussy cat's having himself a time with
that chickenwing," Giselle said. "Lord, you should've
seen Marge jump on a chair that didn't exist and
Francie playing it nonchalant."

Leibush, suddenly, tried to promenade Hcnick and
Winograd back into the steamroom. Unmistakably, he
despaired of certain old-time clients. We had paid to
make the most of things and he, Leibush, saw that he
had no right to ruck and rattle our holdings with a sub-
ordinate tenancy. (Well, never again! Would we forgive
his bad judgement?) Gesticulating, talking in torrents,
he offered his selfishness to both sides as a new discovery
(Come, come, are we such barbarians? Don't resent me,
Ich keniss n't lahd'n. Do you want my tears? Press my
pupik. Please, Judge, no trial. Judge, don't *tsitteh!* If
God establishes the cow He plants the grass. You're in
shvitz, my *panusseh.* It's unavoidable. This place is vine-
less, so Leibush plucks at grapes. And you, Cahoon, the
janitor, with your adaptations, you realist of gill, shell,
hair, and lung. Monkey and mollusk. Janitor! Of these
steamy secrets from Esther, Leibush is the warden. Stay
awhile! And you, Barney Yago, my young neighbor—
are you ashamed of your misfortune? Sit down, spin a
parsol in front of your stump. Provided by the Work-
men's Circle. Colors of the house. In *shvitz* there are no

greenhorns. Who pays attention? A blemish, a potency, in a tub of suds they are indistinguishable. Come, come, find repose. Make a *p'chotik* with me! It's about time we know each other. Who am I? Do you believe I'm that Russian's dog? It's true: I fling my garbage at the sound of bells. Gaw-YIMM! Gaw-YIMM! Sonority of my Carpathian boyhood: a family of seven, watching behind drawn curtains, on a Sunday after Mass. When they passed our house in peace, we knew they'd heard a gentle sermon.) His bitter journey on a milkwhite ass, over moonlit crag and pinnacle, he, the apt observer, into America *goniff*. Every block a toll for Leibush, who shouts back a lingual hemistich. (Sonorous toll, *meineh sunim!* They spit at me! *Mahromurish!* Corrupted *Mudyuh!* Slovak Hunk! *Sziget yuld* on a wooden dish! Am I so bad? Worldwide, they come to me here, in my abode of sheets, beetled and broken, bent for irrigation. From Columbia, Sheriff, Willet and Pitt: tide and panoply. From Ridge, Attorney, and Clinton: cartography of westward tongues. From Suffolk, Norfolk, and Essex: plutocracy of pores, *oysgehtrik'nt!* From Ludlow, Orchard, and Allen: custodians of a tepid scum. From Eldridge, Forsyth and Chrystie: *tink'l ts'lecht,* a goblin chiaroscuro. From Broome and Grand: hawkweed *bolle'gullehs, ubbeh zay darf'n goornit!* From Jackson, Scammel, and Gouverneur: inquisitorial *koptzunim,* their little ones hand in hand. From Jefferson, Rutgers, and Cherry: paladins of crime, taxation. From Water and Monroe: the welshers, else the studious penwipers, *tsimmes* of similitudes. From Madison and Henry and East Broadway: meridian of logic and balloons. They come to me for cleansing, to wheeze and steam in this tropic of Zion, one of a city and two of a family, ratio of chapter and verse, bubbling sap and *zoltz,* shedding their pounds and laconic postils, their antiquities, their whims and fealties, gargalizing *g'mureh*. Blind men and maidens enunciating their ornament. Rhapsodists and diabetics carnal with pronunciamento. Bepearled widows, pink sophomores, myopic out of hermitage. Tenement daughters and continentals, calamitous with dance-hall trivia. *Gabbai* and cop, *ruv* and plucker, traffic specialist and *knubble*—buff, divining a tonic principle. The apprentice in curls, the misanthrope, advised in patronymics. Ida, Reah, *Pinya'mutt'l,* keyed to extremities, special the knees, special the kidney stone, they come to me, one-seventh a *chuchim,* while I proclaim: "In life the best thing is water!")

Leibush had no luck with Henick and Winograd, who, having grown weary of their card game, now showed simple tricks to each other, with little success, since the cards were soggy and unmanageable. Leibush snatched the cards and flung them into the pool. He bent over his cart, picked up a smoked fish, and, affecting a gross ventriloquy, held it alternately over the heads of Henick and Winograd, squealing, bellowing, to ridicule their human talk, modulating his pitch as he changed the position of the shriveled fish, as though all the key centers of derision were natural to his ear. He then held the fish aloft over himself to burlesque his own inventiveness, and he produced a hideous recall of his otherwise pleasant voice, to illustrate the existence of pain in the fish's belly. Ippi, wandering to the far side of the pool, threw a coin into the water, and called out: "Some pipes you got, Leibush—you're a regular Sicilian! Dive deep, you'll find your fortune!"

The girls laughed. The Judge chuckled briefly. Cahoon, in echo, chuckled briefly.

Leibush, almost before we knew it, returned his service cart to an alcove near the locker room. He then
passed swiftly into the steamroom and returned with an
ordinary hose in his hands, which was attached to an unseen tap. Through the steamroom door left ajar, there
came a long scarf of steam, and it hovered at eye-level,
then rose and fanned out under the ceiling. Leibush
pulled the hose taut to the far pool edge. Silent now, and
at peace, he went about the business of cooling his floor
with a certain superiority. But then, straddling his hose,
he cautiously turned the brass nozzle and the stream
came full. He aimed it at the middle of the pool, where
half the cards still floated. and where a polkadot beach-
ball reposed in a watery stasis. The ball was seized and
rotated rapidly upon its axis. For a long while we were
held by the flying polkadots, and the churn of water beneath the ball, as if a sorrow had entered the room and
encircled our heads like a gentle headband. But Leibush
understood that his establishment was no refuge for sorrow; and though he was faced with ten people his
steambath became, in essence, guestless.

So, he turned the hose away from the polkadot ball
and aimed it at Henick and Winograd.

At the moment that the arc of water swerved to hit
him, Winograd suffered an excruciating cramp. He went
forward over the table, this time like a plank breaking
short against its grain. A slight cry came out of him, that
of a child in an echoing place, abiding under the contin-
uing attack from Leibush's hose. It was this child's cry
which informed Henick, who was also being pummeled
and splashed, that this particular cramp was very serious,
more than all the others. Even to us, actual strangers to
the old waiter, the soft, small sound was so ominous that

we were impelled at the same time both to comfort the
man and to escape from him. Winograd, with a twist,
with a jerk, fell off his chair, onto the cement floor, and
lay there waterlogged almost beyond recognition. Leibush had lost momentary control of his hose. He could
not pull it away from its original trajection. On the
floor Winograd was convulsive. But his friend, Henick,
did not move: he was helpless in the memory of the
natural, warm, easy motion to which his friend's body
had always subscribed. Winograd's body had always
walked side by side with his, filled with innocence. Now
the innocence had quit, replaced by a higher sophistica-
tion, which suddenly entered Winograd's nervous system, complete in hardness and angularities, cutting
edges, and tyrannies. Death was pulling a rake across
the elderly flesh, raking away all color, all tone, all
texture of a live companion. Teeth, though false, and
still unpaid for, were stitched together by a thin, cold
thread of fluid. Aged hands and arms were taken by
spasm and agitation. Fingers were spattled with a flaky
pigment, the brow and cheeks broke out in a rash of
fowl-like pores. The corners of his mouth were turned
down, as if by fat, repressive thumbs. The conversion
was total: human body to shattered relic. Only under
the fingernails did a repugnance to finality hang on, a
faint pinkishness, one small sign familiar to life, and, as
his body calmed, his eyes, too, seemed rich with their
lifetime color. Here, in death, was one more lapse, one
more bizarre indulgence to challenge Henick's patience.
All Henick could do was to bring his hands together
again and again, in the idiom of an old understanding,
as if trying to compress a dry loaf of bread, and he kept
on doing this to provide a decent cadence for his friend's
departure.

"Let's get the hell out of here!" Judge Merchant said.

Leibush's hose went wild. We were hit by its stream over and over. It flailed and hacked at us. When I tried to move, my willow limb buckled as my shoe slipped, and sent me down to my knees. I tried, from that position, and under the whacks of water, to move to a more sensible spot. I cannot remember if old Winograd's body lay in the direction of my crawl, or if I was drawn to it because, on hands and knees, I found stirred in myself a quick sense of kinship. The Judge, however, saw in my fall a terrifying delay, since, in his sopping equipage, he was not prepared to deal with this sudden menace. But men know how to go on. And he could only say: "Let's get the hell out of here!"

But I was already at the old waiter's body. I took his head in my hands and began to slap his face. I was not trying to revive him. I knew he was dead. There was no question of revival. The slapping rose out of a secret sense of order. I was destined for order, even in our city. His cheek was gelatinous to my touch, like the meat of a warm plum. And yet, my sense of order drew my lips to his and I blew into his mouth. The Judge said: "If he spits it back I'll scream!"

He ran back and forth, colliding with the others. "No —don't call!—no ambulance!—I mean the police!—do you want to be found here?—oh, this is all so bad!—let's get out of here!"

They ran away. At the moment of our wild separation, I could not persuade my stump and willow limb into a painless balance for flight. Even Leibush had flown; his hose lay whipping on the far side of the pool, shooting water aimlessly, with a soft whistle. The Judge was gone too, holding his head, as though born to have it ultimately severed from its source. Cahoon had flown, which was to be expected, and Ippi too, which I gave no thought, and Kurl, who even prior to Winograd's convulsion had been roaming about hunched-up, his arms half round himself in a cold coil of resignation. The whores had flown too, wilder and faster than the others, since they had to undress and dress again, and gather up their rings and pins, for it was absolutely essential, in view of their occupation, and the unwholesome nature of the situation, to have every last little button for subsequent proof of their never having arrived at all. They dashed out of the locker room, one by one, half dressed, arms laden, and they made for the street, each, in the end, in solitude.

When all was quiet I sat and stared at the dead waiter. The room was now full of shadows of fagends of steam still floating through the steamroom door. The whistling hose provided the only sound. Finally, I searched for a phone, found it, and called the police.

Formal observances and queries were made. It was Winograd's heart . . . that, at least, was ascertained by the responding Bellevue physician. Owing to the hour, and to the repetitiveness of such cases in our precinct, the ceremony was little more than mechanical. Was there a priest who should be informed? He was a Jew. I watched them carry him away.

At nine on Thursday morning I met Bibber in our hall. He had already heard of Winograd's death. He regretted the cold which had kept him away from the steambath. To Bibber—who knew of the old waiter's bad heart, his blood pressure—his death did not come as a surprise.

"Another one gone," he said. "So . . . one person less to suffer. Henick is next on the list . . . you'll see!"

Nor did the flight of Judge Merchant and company astound him.

"Listen to me . . . Winograd is dead from his appetite. His appetite came from waiting too long for God to take him. It proves that a man can dig his own grave just with his mouth. As for that bunch of *gonuvim* running out on you . . . in their place I would run too! After all, to save his good will an American will go out and kill himself!"

He chuckled. He slipped his hand under his beard and wagged it at me like a ruminating goat. Then he pushed the beard straight out.

"What do you expect, closing yourself up in your rooms for so many years like an old pair of pants on a hanger? People have a right to run out on you! Stop thinking about Winograd! He's just plain dead Winograd. Another old man who dropped dead one night in our beautiful city. Like I will. Like you will." He laughed again.

I waved him away and left him.

An old waiter's death had become linked to my conscience. I went to my rooms and put the twenty dollars into an envelope, which I addressed to Ippilito. Then I went to bed.

PART THREE

FRIDAY

FRIDAY NOON, CAHOON KNOCKED AT MY DOOR.
Facing him, I caught again the scent of our halls, that
mingling of cabbage and St. John's bread.

He licked his lips and touched his eyepatch as another
man would tip his hat.

"D'you know, Mr. Yago, we had more light in these
halls when we were usin' naptha jets."

I went back into my rooms for the envelope and gave
it to him without explanation. When he saw Ippilito's
name on it, and the dark tones of money through it, he
said: "Ah, well, Mr. Yago, every man serves his own
master."

The scent of our halls was powerful and stubborn. It
filled my head, my lungs. It was low and hovering; it
clung to his scurfy black hat like a noxious gas.

He, too, had trouble with it.

"Somebody must be puttin' up pickles, Mr. Yago.
D'you smell the cloves?"

"No."

"You don't? It's the damn three-day mist, y'know. It

won't let the natural odors out of the building. But I'd swear there's a hint of the odor of cloves today."

"I smell no cloves."

"Well, it's about the time of the year Mrs. Tartock puts up her bushel of pickles, isn't it? I also get a bit of a smoky wick in the air. D'you?"

"Neither cloves nor candles, Mr. Cahoon."

"D'you suppose somebody's lightin' one of them glass memorials? What d'you call them?"

"*Yahrzeit* candles."

"D'you suppose maybe that's what's doin' it?"

"Is there something special you wanted from me?"

"There bloody goddam well is and I'm not one to make the stink of this lovely affair easy on you nor anyone else, for that matter, leastways myself!"

"What affair?"

"Mr. Yago! That bloody bum of an eggcandler was right after all! C'n you put that little misunderstandin' down at Suffolk Street out of your mind?"

"It's forgotten."

"Well if you c'n stand the livin' truth about your old pal Bibber, I want you to come along with me, Mr. Yago, I just want you to come alone with me!"

He pulled his hat from his head and threw it against a wall. Then he kicked it down the stairs.

"Imagine! Imagine Esther givin' suck to that bloody abomination!"

He slammed at his thigh with his hand, and lurched and stomped in front of my door.

"And I want you to make a mental note of things and write it down in your goddam book!"

He slammed again at his thigh. He wheeled round in a dance, as if he could no longer endure the emotion which drove him to my door.

"Mr. Poetical Yago! D'you think you're livin' in a bowl of seashells?"

He pulled a blue, dotted workman's rag out of his pocket, and twirled it overhead.

"What do I look like, Mr. Yago? Hah! An old Jew *shloogen kopoory?* Now how does it go? Old Bibber once explained it to me! Atone with the fowl on Yom Kippur morn . . . male persons take a rooster, female ones a hen . . . a pregnant woman takes both, a rooster and a hen! Death for the chicken and life for me! . . . Death for the chick and life for the mick!"

He kept twirling the dotted rag overhead.

"And Bibber is captain over the Zamzum—mims! Distress them not nor meddle! I mean business, Mr. Yago!"

Then he snapped the rag at me in contempt.

"Here it is right under your nose and you won't believe it . . . distress them not nor meddle . . . oh, Jesus!"

Once more he snapped his dotted rag at me.

"Who the hell do they think I am—a bloody Jerusalem landlord in a single-breasted suit?"

And then he started toward the stairs. His rag kept snapping in the air like a battle flag.

"Mr. Yago! Would you give nuts in a punnet to a toothless man if you knew he'd be too damn polite to say no? Now come along with me, Mr. Poetical Author, and I'll give you one sweet peep at a giant of a man!"

I followed him down the stairs. He stopped for his hat, and jammed it on his head. He remembered that I was able to manage only one step at a time, and he waited. He sent up a column of babble into which I descended.

"Hah! They'll gobble up their own heads one fine day, mark my words. Oh, they think they're so bloody sen-

sible! Imagine them usin' a child . . . imagine them
usin' a child!"

His voice caused an occasional door to open, and
frightened eyes to appear. At the sight of Cahoon, the
doors banged shut.

"If I never did give the kid the time she deserved,
neither did I ever call her a fat little tub. Never once a
bit of criticism, or, what do they call it, renunciation?
After all, she's only here on a foster arrangement, don't
y'know? Jesus, they think they're so bloody sensible!"

He reached his landing. Spinning to face me, he
pointed a finger at me, to mark his tenderness for those
who are victimized for no particular sin.

"Cahoon the dumb Mick janitor. Damn, it's so bloody
hard to find the words! Who other than me the Mick
would walk that child down Clinton Street after school
where she loves them bridal windows? Who but me the
Mick saw the little eyes fill up at sight of them gorgeous
mannequins, and them ribbon bouquets and them little
white hats? Who but the Mick knew what went on in
that little girl's head? Who but the Mick? Christ, why
should them mannequins be more gorgeous in life than
she herself who breathed?"

At Mildred Osot's door, he stopped, and said: "Osot's
in a coma, did y'know that?"

At Quastafesti's door, he stopped and said: "I always
get a whiff of the seaweed right here, d'you?"

Cahoon had a key to the rooms adjoining his own.
We went in. Here lived the Polido sisters, who were bus-
girls at the automat. Their rooms were littered with
newspapers and religious objects; also unclean dishes
and shopping lists.

"I hear they're both pregnant," Cahoon said.

"How do you know that?"

"Well, if they're not it's allright with me."

In the tight, dark little entryway, I bruised my thigh on a corner of an old sewing machine. This entryway also served as a wardrobe. Cahoon worked the sewing machine out from under the hems of garments. There was barely room for either of us between those woolen walls of large buttons and dangling belts.

"We're going to stand on this," Cahoon said. "It'll hold."

"Are we allowed in here?"

"I suspect a leak in the walls and I'm here to investigate. You're kindly lending a hand."

He piled one wall of garments on the floor. With the woolens disturbed the air was musty. Cahoon moved the sewing machine where it would serve to his advantage. I did not offer to help him. In these tight quarters he was not troubled by our forced intimacy, though he was concerned with noise.

"I say it for a fact, Mr. Yago, a young Irishman should never marry. Too many fights and revolutions and things of importance to get started. To hell with it!"

A band of tin panels joined the walls to the ceiling. Many of them were rusted, and had twisted free of the wall studs. Cahoon folded a panel in; it crimped at the joint but he settled it sufficiently with a flat hand. He now had a window, through which he gazed.

I tried to steady the sewing machine on which he stood, but he waved his arms, hovering over me like a six-winged angel. He talked rapidly in a whisper. Whatever it was that he saw caused his hand to beat against his thigh.

"Ah! . . . ah! . . . ah, Mr. Yago, my God! He's not even a goddam citizen!"

"Hold still, Mr. Cahoon, this thing is shaky."

"From the very beginnin' I should have known! D'you know when he first come into this buildin' he was brought in by a man from HIAS—that Jewish outfit. Esther and me were in the kitchen. We both raised an eyebrow over the way he rattled off that good English. And d'you know the first bloody thing he said to me? Well, I'd just given Esther a little birthday gift, a pretty little slave chain for round the ankle from Golino the credit jeweler down on Avenue B. I've never forgotten a birthday yet, I assure you! Anyway, I asked him what he liked most about our country that he could tell about in such a short time—and he said our slave chains for women! Imagine it bein' the bloody first thing he laid eyes on steppin' into our kitchen! Now he did not want to insult us, neither Esther nor myself, he says, but he'd been noticing slave chains all over the bloody shop. Esther's as vain as the next woman, mind you, and she turned three kinds of red, and stuck the old leg out just a shade more. You'd swear even the ankle blushed. It reminded him of another little chain, he says, not gold, mind you, nor half so pretty nor delicate, but a slave chain all the same. Not to hurt us, he says, nor spoken in any bitterness, but the other little chain was strung across the seal of a boxcar that he and his family road across Poland in. On a one-way excursion, he says. In America, he says, these pretty little chains under a sheer silk stocking gave him a feelin' that every refugee wants to come to America for the wrong reasons! C'n you imagine the underhandedness of a person? Speakin' like that to a man in the presence of his wife? C'n you imagine a man who just come through such holy hell layin' eyes the bloody first thing on Esther's leg? Ah, my God, come on up here, Mr. Yago, I want you to see this!"

. . .

"The blessedness of a marriage contract and a bit of Yiddish decency, that's what you're in for!"

Our weight was supported by pressing in on the wall. We also held fast to the rim of our little window. In this way the sewing machine remained quite steady, and jiggled only when Cahoon, trying to subdue his vehemence, broke into spasms of whispering.

Each time he regained his balance he insisted that I study his posture, since he had experimented previously in these tight quarters, and had made of the procedure a personal skill.

The wall was a common one between the Polido entryway and the janitor's kitchen, and through the window I saw Bibber seated at the Cahoon table, that solid oaken wheel set on half a keg.

Bibber was alone. His eyes alternated between an open book before him and the crinoline bedroom curtains, which served as the bedroom door, behind which there was a stirring of small noises, mutterings, and jarcap sounds. Bibber rose and walked to the grimyglass turtle-tank, atop the fake mantelpiece. He chinked at the glass with his fingernail. On the bed of pink stones nothing would crawl. Bibber peered from above into the tank.

"Pheh! *S'shtinkt!*"

Esther laughed behind the curtain, and was joined in laughter by little Jenny.

"Ah, Christ, the bloody vulgar lot of them!" Cahoon said.

Trembling now, he hung on stubbornly. Our two chins on the sill of his dismal window seemed to him entirely prudent. "Bibber, dear," Esther called from the bedroom, "how would you go about koshering a turtle?"

Bibber chuckled. "Take out the vein!"

Cahoon dabbed at his lips with his dotted rag. "I have one choice," he said, "I can slit my throat or slit his!"

Behind the curtain something fell clattering to the floor.

"That's our dainty little Jenny for you!" Esther called out.

Cahoon began to rock back and forth. His lips moved over a muted babble. He let go of the jagged rim and covered his face with his hands. I suspected that he was mocking a Jew in prayer. He had begun to sob. The sewing machine swayed. I patted his shoulder, not to comfort him, but to remind him of our precarious footing. He took hold of the rim again. He seemed unaware that I was still at his side, participating in the same clandestine watch. He went on quietly sobbing, and dabbing at his lips, gesturing in despair at his kitchen, at the tumid and molested corpse of his once happy marriage.

The curtains parted. Little Jenny came out of the bedroom and moved shyly to Bibber at the oaken wheel. In every detail, to the last brightly colored feather and bead, she was a perfect miniature of Esther Cahoon's sorrowful wooden Indian! Bibber was so pleased that he bent forward and kissed the girl's cheek, settling back with a greasepaint smear on his beard.

"Look at that fishface!" Cahoon said. "Look how gay he is! He's as bright as a sturgeon's bladder!"

Little Jenny, all plump and red in buckskin and sandals, nervous, shy, and ready to giggle, began a recitation.

"Sha! Sha! . . . wait for your mother," Bibber said.

"Sure, sure," Cahoon whispered, "stick with the winner, you wise old *yidl*. And she's not the kid's mother!"

Cahoon stopped sobbing. He was, in fact, quite sure of himself, transfigured. This clandestine perch was now a bar of honor on which to declaim his present hardship!

When his wife walked through their curtain to join little Jenny, he nodded and sighed, to reveal his pain, and the weight of his debasement. When he became aware of my eyes on his profile, he smiled: a smile of generosity before this terrible default of trust.

In buckskin and bright feather headdress both Esther and little Jenny now stood before Bibber, who applauded softly. She pouted for Bibber, as she had pouted for me on Monday past, confirming his captivity. She bristled in his delight. Little Jenny, attentive upon her foster mother, also pouted.

"Do you like her costume?" Esther asked of Bibber.

"It's beautiful!"

"It gave me so much pleasure to make. I used the sewing machine next door—the Polido girls are away all day and I'd go right in and sew with their kind permission. It wasn't too easy—I mean, to figure everything down in size—the headpiece and sandals were the worst, but I don't think all the material together ran me three dollars!"

"Esther, my dear, I must tell you, it's beautiful! Does she know the song? Well, you've rehearsed long enough. No? Dear Esther, you shouldn't be embarrassed. I mean, you look so ashamed. You should only be ashamed when something is ugly. What you've got here is beautiful. Do you know that you are a gifted seamstress? *Ki hinay chayi 'reya biyod hawro 'kaym* (Lo! as drapery in the hands of the embroiderer!) and you, Jenny, in the history of your country there has never been such a juicy little Indian!"

"It's a good idea, isn't it? Jenny and me together? It *is* a good idea, isn't it?"

"Esther, dear, only God . . . *l'goleh amuƙoys ba'din* (Who revealeth the depths of judgment), can say what is good in the future and what is not good. To a plain neighbor, it's beautiful."

"Then you give us the signal when you're ready!"

Bibber closed the book he had been reading and removed his fur-wheel *shtrom'l* from his head and placed it over the book. Immediately he put on a black skullcap. He snapped his fingers in the air.

"SH'MA! SH'MA KOLENU! SH'MA AMERICA!"

"Alright, sweetheart," Esther said to the child, "watch me!"

"Chata'emu   chat'ey   b'ndibas   g'shmecha!" Bibber prayed.

Esther and little Jenny, though without comprehension, were lifted up by Bibber's call for their words to be heard by the ears of our country, and their errors to be cleansed by a liberal rain. Their shyness was redeemed in his call. His gestures, his voice, in which they found a powerful praise and tenderness, had beckoned them to sorrow, and love, and magical beauty. An excitement entered Esther's bosom; she shivered. It moved little Jenny to brandish a toy tomahawk over a hundred imaginary scalps.

"Not yet, sweetheart, wait for me!" Esther said.

Bibber waved his hand in a small arc, and took them into his grace, his gentleness. Proudly they entered their new existence, their superexistence, each to the other in fit proportion, a large block of wood and a small one, solidifying before Bibber's eyes—two marvels of control, rising, rising, to giant heights. Esther out of her perpetual bosom, little Jenny out of her tubbiness, two wooden

Indians transcending ancestral hazards, rose over the
oaken wheel, their kitchen, Tenth Street, rose over all
their particular penances, freezing with perfection only
to alter perniciously, to moan over their corrupted
strains, their desecration, until eyes flicked, fingers
twitched, arms shot out in spasms, and the war dance
came. Toy tomahawks swung in cadence. Sweet smiles
defended the bloodletting. Two thankless planks, vile
and low and pathetic, abundant in human feeling, menacing Bibber with their hatchets, began to sing:

> ". . . No rage are we from the Osage
> Unspoken by Spokane
> The Erie, Seneca, or Naskapi
> Deny our stamping by a pappy.
> Just look at us! Just look at us!
> Two hearts forever misunderstood
> And all because they throb in wood."

Bibber pounded at the oaken wheel as I had pounded a hatbox—FLOOSH BAM WHUMP WHUMP
WHUMP.

"Oh forgive their abomination!" he yelled, throwing
up his arms, *"Slach naw g'yulum v'yichyu m'mkoyr
imecha!* (And grant them life from thy fountain!)

Little Jenny was excellent. Even Cahoon was surprised by her gifts for mimicry. He nudged me repeat-
edly to notice her smallest move. She had memorized
every crease of expression modeled by Esther. She also
echoed her model's maturer enunciations, and cleverly
slurred the difficult words, such as "Algonquin and Susquehanna," and she danced with her model through
their wooden chambers of love, of sorrow and innocence. Beads clacked, sandals slapped, feathers quivered.
Bibber was given over entirely to their mournful song,

and the little girl's voice. He suffered with them their impassive destiny. No matter how shattering their plea he could not release them from their doom. He was at once intoxicated and degraded by this doom. Tears came to his eyes. He wept for his wooden Indians, for his own poor scalp, for the slave chain round Esther's ankle, and for this beloved little Jenny who strove so mightily to please him; he wept for her immovable turtles on their bed of pink stones, our building, our street, our neighbors. He wept for America. He wept for his own weeping.

> ". . . Shawnee, Pawnee, Huron, Oto,
> Modoc, Chinook, and Papago. . . ."

FLOOSH . . . WHUMP . . . BAM . . . BAM . . . BAM

"For all these, O God of forgiveness, forgive us, pardon us, grant us remission!"

> ". . . The Pueblo, the Nootka, the fiery Mingo
> One and all debase our lingo. . . ."

"Al cheyt shecha'tawnu l'fawnecha b'lautzoyn. (For the sin of our scoffing.)

> ". . . Just look at us, just look at us,
> Two souls in hell who thirst for good,
> Two spirits in darkness who shiver in wood."

Bibber jumped up. He took Esther and the child by the hand. *"SH'MA! SH'MA!"*

He joined their rythmic war dance. They circled the oaken wheel, and kept going round it, chanting.

They were beside themselves. Bibber wept and laughed. His emotion touched the beseeching Indians, and they wildly repeated verses and mixed them up.

Soon there was a coalescence of song and prayer from
bursting hearts in presumably human voices. Cahoon's
kitchen now rang with a reeling litany! . . . A Sioux, a
Ute, a Crow, a Cree . . . Yea, faithful art thou to
quicken the dead! . . . Defiles the Cheyenne, the Seneca tree. . . . *B'ruch atau adonoy m'chayeh hameysim.*
. . . Seminole hearts which shiver in wood. . . . .
Blessed art thou, O Lord, who quickenest the dead!"

They held fast to each other, leaping round the table.
Once, the child broke away, and menaced both Esther
and Bibber with lethal swipes of her tomahawk. They
kept going, as if each, in delirium, would not be outdone
by the other. But soon the chanting subsided into a melancholy hum. Finally, in exhaustion, their reel ended.
And in one sheer upward leap little Jenny sprang to
Bibber. With her arms round his neck she hung on to
him, while he embraced her and spun her in a declining
torque of feathers.

Little Jenny covered Bibber's face with kisses. She
brandished her tomahawk overhead.

"Halleluye, halleluye, Jenny! My Jenny! praise Him!
Z'ḳaynim im'nurim. (Old men and children.)"

They fell together onto the bench and the child played
the tomahawk on his cheek.

"Let me shave you, Uncle Bibber."

"Sweetheart, for this beard you'd need a regular chop-
per."

She slid from his lap and sank to the floor at his feet,
reposing there happily. In breathlessness, Bibber's whole
body heaved and pitched. He rejoiced. His fingertips
transferred a kiss from his own lips to the child's.

"*Emes v'yatziv* (True and firm)," he said. "*V'naw-
choyn v'ḳayum* (established and enduring, right and
faithful, beloved and precious, desirable and pleasant)."

．　．　．

His beard and face were mottled with citron smudges. Esther came to him. She tried to mold the accidental smudges into facial coins. Bibber bent toward her. He lifted his face to lighten her task. But his mood had changed. He fidgeted with his Willkie-button ear, and propped up his beard. (A face abounding in beard . . . a nose with a juiceless boil!)

Esther would not spare him. Nor herself. She had both hands to his face, to his cheeks especially, to rub him out of his medium nature into the most muscular of young warriors! She rubbed and molded. Bibber held his hand up to calm her, to let her know it was preposterous. But she had jumped with delight into the possibility! She asked him to open his mouth, then to close it; to look stern, then fierce, then peaceful, then energetic, then hungry, then triumphant. He abided her every wish, hoping to achieve an expression to check her foolishness. But Esther went on; she soared into imaginary realms of purity. And when Bibber tried to catch her hand, she rebuffed him, and scolded: Close your eyes! Sit straight, now bend, now turn, sit up, absolutely up!

"This is going to be darn good!" she said.

Bibber sank, his shoulders sagged, his head was yielded up for her to do what she liked with it. He had failed to make known his embarrassment, or to turn her gaze toward the enormity of her error.

Esther could not even respond to little Jenny, who had begun to pluck at her feathers for attention. And when she finished, she retired to study her handiwork, wiping her hands on a dishrag. She studied and pondered. Bibber, all mottle and smudge, his beard flashing with color, his skullcap slashed by citron streaks, elevated his Willkie-button ear to catch her words, should any come. He was searching for some encouragement, some congenial word of hope! At some point in her work he had begun to regard his transformation seriously!

Little Jenny rose from the floor and joined Esther in examining Bibber. Without a word they stared at him. He sat very still, waiting. (Ah, well, at its worst it was only a poor joke.)

As she stood before him, the child's feather coronal slipped awry, and Bibber reached out to correct it. The child laughed. She stepped backward, stiffly putting him off. Esther, too, was now stiffened by this bearded, bewildering being concocted by her own hand. She remained wordless, her expression cold and flat. She began to fret her own cheeks. To Bibber her eyes were blank. He felt nothing but her coldness; for a moment winter had come into her kitchen, and froze his beard, his hands, his nose. She drew her little Jenny close to her side.

They gazed somberly at old Bibber, in whom they'd hoped to situate some final approbation. Everything about him looked so noticeable now! He had never showed his age so much! She should have known, but who could have known? And now, under her own headpiece of feathers, she despaired at her mistake. Imagine trying to arouse in Bibber a primitive barbarism to which she might be enslaved!

"My God!" she said. She gestured toward him: a parent toward a cretinous child. Then, she slowly removed her feathers and carried them to Bibber. Painstakingly, she worked them down over his skullcap, and fitted them on his head.

"Esther, please," Bibber said.

"Well, look at you, kid."

"Esther, dear, what kind of a Chinook would I make?"

Bibber rose and stood before them.

"Papage or Seneca—what is he, Jenny, dear?"

"It's crazy!" the child cried out.

Bibber plucked at his Willkie-button ear, with an almost feminine grace, and without shyness.

"Well? Don't you want to teach me the song? Come, we'll do the little dance! Jenny, dear, give me your hatchet!"

"No! It's crazy. It's no good!"

"Come, Jenny, come take my hand. Let me have it. Don't you want me to be a Chinook Huron Susquehanna?"

"It's no good, it's no good!"

Bibber laughed. He shook his head wildly. His feathers quivered and rustled as he went into a gay ambit round the oaken wheel. Up and down he danced, the most felicitous of painted warriors. He reveled in a new sense of fellowship with these tribal women. But the child began to cry.

"It's so crazy . . . it's no good . . . I hate you! it's crazy!"

Bibber wagged his finger under Esther's nose. She was incapable of movement. His headpiece snapped and whooshed; the train of feathers snapped at his heels.

"Why are you laughing, Esther? Or is it that you're crying? Do you think you have a reasonable complaint? Oh, I know why you're laughing! Out of satisfaction with my self-respect. No? Then you're really crying! Are you afraid that I'm such competition? But look at me! Hi! Hi! And my little dance Hi! Hi! Then you're not crying? You must be crying. Ah, so it's little Jenny who must be laughing. Of course, a child of God cannot be fooled! She knows that God has no ambitions for Bibber, and yet Bibber has ambitions for God! It's true what that Yago says, I'm an ancient creaky old Jew! Esther, I'm telling you this child has the gift of God's laughter. You and I . . . well, we're at home in our stupidity, but this child has the gift of laughter! Can't you see it? Certainly you see it!"

"You smell!" little Jenny cried out to him.

"You see? Esther, did you hear that? I smell! Do I really smell? So, Leibush has a customer! Do I really smell? Only now you've discovered it? I'm a Nootka, how can I smell?"

"You do! You do! It's no good! It's crazy!"

"How can I smell? I'm a naked American Nootka with red skin. Look, naked to the bone. Hi! Hi! Let's begin the dance! I'm one hundred percent a citizen. Esther, dear, look how you're blushing! Listen to your little Jenny! I smell! Now you know with what goodness everybody but Bibber the Nootka lives in our beautiful house! Hi! Hi! hi! the beggar, hi! the fool, I grab a tickle in the *shool!* Everybody but Bibber the Chinook Huron, Susquehanna. The smell is only Bibber's. Hi! Hi!"

His ambit round the oaken wheel took full force. His arms flailed, his feathers snapped. The child leaped toward him. She kicked at him, and swung her hatchet at his face, and pounded at his chest with her little fist. She flung her whole being at Bibber so wantonly that Esther was finally driven to speak: "Jenny! Stop it! Have you lost your head?"

"I hate him! He don't smell good!"

Bibber hit the child hard across the face. He hit her again.

"Enough!" he said.

He then took hold of the child's ear, and pinched it, and, by means of gripping the lobe, held her off at a distance.

"*Bashauma'yim uvau'auretz!* In heaven and earth, Jenny, you will pay attention. I've had enough! And you must tell that to your Esther, and your Cahoon, and Barney Yago, the fancy storyteller, and everybody in the building, and all the children on the block! Bibber has had enough! And now let me tell you something! You're a little girl whose nose is always running . . . and when you've got brains enough to carry your own handkerchief, you won't have to listen to me, but now you must listen to me. There were once three men— Dosa, Ishmael, and Eleazer. And Dosa said that children's talk, together with being in the house of the ignorant, will put an old man like me out of the world. Ishmael was smart, too, and he said be submissive to a superior and receive all men with cheerfulness. Ask your Esther what that means! And when it comes to Eleazer, he said, where there is no Torah there are no manners. Where there are no manners there is no Torah. That's why I've had enough! Do you know what the Torah is? It's a big book!"

Little Jenny, in a convulsion of sobs and tears, rubbed her ear when Bibber released it. She turned away from him. She also turned away from Esther. She had no further need for her model of deportment.

Bibber, calm now, and assured, gently lifted the feather headpiece off his head, careful not to dislodge his skullcap. He came to Esther and paused before her. And then he recrowned her with her own bright feather coronal. He shook his head at her, and then a finger. He took the dishrag from her hands, wiped his face clean of smudges of greasepaint. Again he shook a finger—no more pranks, the finger said, no more injurious pranks!

Esther would not budge. This familiar finger-shaking she could not tolerate. Cahoon himself was a finger shaker, and Bibber's kept going in the velocity of its previous claims.

"Educate the child," he said to her. "Educate the child!"

"It's innocent!" Cahoon said. "Mr. Yago! It's so bloody allfire innocent!"

We were hurrying out of the Polido rooms.

"But you wouldn't think the old gentleman would strike a kid, though she deserved it with her fresh mouth! But still he had no right to strike the kid! If it wouldn't give me away he'd get a headful from this old Mick, you can bet on that!"

I pushed him aside. "Go away, Mr. Cahoon."

"Just the same, you've got to give the devil his share. The kid was damn good as a pint-size Indian. Of course, it'll never come to anythin'. Still, it keeps them out of mischief. It's a way to get acquainted, I mean Esther and the kid. Wouldn't you say so? What d'you think I ought to do?"

"It's a free country. Do what you like."

"Well, I'll let it slide. Best thing all round. I'm not one to see the worst in people. I look for the best in people—don't put on airs and be good to the poor. It's the sensible way, Mr. Yago. It's only performin' a function of the Church, and I'm not bein' facetious!"

He pulled a slip of paper out of his pocket and waved it under my nose. "By the way, Mr. Yago, I forgot to give you your receipt on Mondy mornin'."

SATURDAY

ᚱᕀᕀ ON SATURDAY MORNING I HEARD THAT MILDRED OSOT'S husband was dead. In front of her door there was a crush of neighbors. I pushed my way in. Her rooms were furnished with familiar futilities, though every stick and shred was polished and cleaned, which only served to betray their shabbiness.

She sat upright in a yellow kitchen chair, this phthisic, unknitted figure with warm and impish eyes. All round her hovered her neighbors, changing guard with much ostentation and couching of sympathy. Her eyes were now almost blood-red under her compress of gray hair. Her earrings no longer looked comical, nor did she give in to that stooped concavity with which we were all familiar. She seemed in excellent control of herself. Having waited nine months for a higher authority than herself to release her Osot from his konchur, she was quite certain that she had ushered him to his resting place with proper ceremony.

I paid my respects. She nodded. Cahoon pushed his way through. He bent toward her.

"Today no sugra burn, Mister."

"Not today, Mrs. Osot, dear—maybe tomorrow."

Bibber came by, and Leibush, and Bailey the sodaman. Bibber gave her a word, and turned immediately, pushing his way out.

In the small room there was much repressed motion under a muting of dialects. When called on, our neighbors could become insensate with sympathy, just as if it was greed. Ironically, Mildred Osot spurred them on, for she sat in her chair so benignly that her callers were deeply embarrassed. Even the bachelor Golino brothers, two old glazers, cousins to the credit-jeweler on Avenue B, even these two old bachelors who lived on the ground floor, who had never concealed their contempt for Mildred and her purifying bowl of sugar, came by to extend their condolences. Widow and callers, neighbors and friends, were unified in commiseration. Bazer, our druggist, was also there. Quastafesti had once described him as a "pitiful old mule with a full nose, who still hungers for elegance after forty-one years on Avenue C, as evidenced in the way he wraps those ancient powders for heartburn!"

Still, in the press of mourners, Bazer, who was also our public notary, was quite composed, and attuned, though the pockets of his coat were stuffed with paper and cord, and his eyeglasses were joined together by dirty adhesive tape. He had come in at first as a comrade and brother; then, perceiving that the very force of his quietude had made his presence sufficiently felt by all, he became as an amanuensis in a meeting of vassals, there to declaim for the widow our tithe of tears. Out of an important-looking brown envelope he took an official paper. He showed it round; it was judiciously notarized with red wax and seal, and a snip of blue ribbon. The document quickly attracted our neighbors by its bona fide authority, and a gradual stillness came over them; they were now gathered in the most rarified of atmospheres.

Bazer saw a nearly central position at Mildred's chair from which to speak and moved to it. He held up his hand. He began to read from his notarized document, in a voice so touched by this self-appointed chore that many callers moaned quietly, especially when they heard their own names gratuitously assigned to this panegyric.

"I, Anton Bazer, of the State of New York, of the City and County of New York, being duly sworn, do depose, and do say, that the following names hereunto affixed are true of my own knowledge, sworn to before me this date, and that the following wish this paper to be a token, to Mrs. Osot, of 921 East 10th Street, of the Borough of Manhattan, Second District Municipal Court of the City of New York, of their heartfelt loss together with her own, on the departure of her husband! Mrs. Valentine Bramovitch for herself and her husband Valentine in his illness; Miss Jenny Danziger, for her foster-parents Mr. and Mrs. Stanley Cahoon; Mr. and Mrs. Aza Luft; Victor Propish; Mr. and Mrs. John Helm in remembrance of their son, Yutchie; Mr. and Mrs. August Turino; Anthony Quastafesti for his children Vincent and Gilda; Israel and Gretta Marks; Miss Yetta Nostrand; Misses Gina and Doris Zwar; Mr. and Mrs. Leo Costa; Mr. and Mrs. Victor Puente; Mr. and Mrs. Francis Wellerky; Judge Jesse Merchant; Mr. Harry Ippilito; Esther Cahoon in remembrance of her mother, Zena Cudcik; Mr. Aaron Bibber; Mr. Elias Kipler; Mr. Julius Leibush; Mr. Martin Bailey; Mr. Herman Tepp; Mr. and Mrs. Andrew Tartock; Mr. Constantin Vogel; Mrs. Paul Taffy; Mr. Eddie Chen; Mr. Frederick Abibal and daughters; Mr. Horace Silvestre; Mr. Louis Alverez; Mr. Jesus Martinez; Evelyn and Judy Polido."

Bazer said thank you to the callers, his voice full of feeling, and he handed the paper to Mildred Osot, and departed without another word.

There was a commotion at the door. Lucy Tartock had brought with her a bowl of pickled herring and a loaf of bread. Several women barred her entry. While

Osot was still laid out at Frugelli's, the mortician at Twelfth and Avenue A, Mildred's chambers were as yet consecrate, and the passing of food over the threshold would have been a defilement.

Mrs. Tartock, because of her husband's night hours, had long ago come to find our calendar unintelligible, and she stood to the simple succession of our days as a child toward time, an uninformed consciousness in relation with the perpetual motion of light and dark. Mrs. Wellerky tried to make it known to her that Osot had died yesterday and would be buried tomorrow, at which time it would be proper to bring in food for the post-funeral callers. This information was too ambiguous. The fact that Osot was above and not below the ground shocked Mrs. Tartock, for she had heard such a long time ago of his death. In the dismal hall Mrs. Wellerky detained her under a stern instruction of dates and hours, but for Mrs. Tartock they were hypotheses impossible to verify, and she stood on the spot quietly, clutching her bowl and loaf, an enigmatically sedate woman with red eyes. She looked, in fact, as if she had inherited her husband's chronic conjunctivitis. Mrs. Wellerky talked, Mrs. Tartock listened. In her displacement she came to stand very still, and straight, as if straightness alone was the perfect form of neighborliness . . . but I knew it to be a paralysis with respect to her place in the daylight hours. And when she moved, she turned in a curious way, in a cautious spin on one heel! She had placed her loaf across the plate-lid of her bowl, which she now held with only one hand. Something in her was aroused. It was a strange sight. She was so rarely dislodged from her own rooms before dark, I suspected that the breach itself had further disordered her grasp on externals. And then, having had enough, she tried to elevate the bowl while she turned! The divinity that shaped the end of Osot must have made itself known to her, for she seemed determined to ritualize this bowl aloft, high above her head while she continued to show us all her sides. The bowl was too heavy, she could not sustain it, and down it came: bowl, plate-lid, and loaf of bread, smashing to the floor.

Before anybody could check her, Mildred Osot was out in the hall, sloshing toward her neighbor through herring chunks and peppercorns, through onion rings and bayleaf, sailing downstream toward the stairs on a milky river of brine. (This river was the source of an eventual odor which was to cling to our walls for nine days.) Mildred knew of Mrs. Tartock's mania for cleanliness, and had come rushing out to soften the poor woman's humiliation, and while Mrs. Wellerky tried to coax the widow back into her trap to resume her sorrowful watch, and while other women dashed toward neighboring doors for mops and rags, Mildred Osot embraced Lucy Tartock at the foot of the landing, now an estuary into which floated quart upon quart of pickling brine.

They both wept. They were lashed to each other. In their sorrow they kissed. Each thanked the other for her goodness, her thoughts. Mildred apologized for the denseness of those women at her door who had rebuffed Mrs. Tartock's act of kindness. She begged her to come into her rooms and take an equal place with all the others. She begged her not to unduly efface herself because of this little accident. By the smell alone she knew that Mrs. Tartock's herring was delicious! Osot himself, prior to his konchur, had been our building's supreme eater of pickled herring, and Mildred was now certain that God's fist had knocked the bowl out of Lucy's hand, for look! look! look where it was all running!—down the stairs, down into the streets, down deep under the muddy gutter where Osot will go tomorrow to savor its excellence in peace among the heavy stones!

"Come, lady," Mrs. Osot said to her, "come in my rooms, don't listen to womens stupid womens. Osot vurk down bank. He leave me money! I pay you back for luffly herrings make! Sure, sure, you poor womens, you not lose money. I pay you for herrings make!"

Our neighbors were resentful. In whispers they raked the queer Mrs. Tartock through, and I left them to their business.

I went down and into the street for fresh air. I roamed the neighborhood until nightfall. I walked, and worked the babble out of my ears. Winter had returned; not a trace was left of the previous three-day mist. On Szold Place the fumes of a burning tire filled my nose. I thought of how Osot's death would forever fill my nose in the form of an odor of pickling brine. And I thought of the triad of deaths that had filled my head since Monday morning—Zena Cudcik, Winograd, Osot.

Quastafesti had once likened our city to a giant stalk, from which its creatures fell like bananas, one by one, green or ripe, it did not matter.

That night I visited with Bibber. It had turned very cold. Cahoon again economized on coal—our walls were glazed with frost. The air in Bibber's kitchen abounded in our steamy breathballs. We shivered and ground our teeth, and had no desire to move for the rest of the night.

About Osot's death, Bibber said: "He's better off!"

About Lucy Tartock's moment at Mildred's door, he said: "I can smell pickled herring like anybody else—some smell!"

"By now it's a stink."

"I'm not yet a citizen. How can I say it's a stink?"

For me, his kitchen's remorseless cold had invested the odor of brine with a hint of the odor of war—not the smoke, nor the metallic whiff of an ejected shell, nor even the odor of a human corpse, but simply the smell of litter, of things of life abandoned, of ruined things and wreckage, which covered the fields and roads as I walked them before I lost my leg.

For lack of another subject, Bibber and I went on about stinks. He argued that our hall had an enduring and characteristic stink, just as our city had a stink, enduring and deep. The stink of our city was American, while the stink of our halls was European. I argued that both hall and city stinks were the same, one, a universal stink, a stink of death ever-present. He accused me of an idiotic nose; Europe might very well stink of death, while in America it was not death but ignorance which stank, compounded in our halls by the stink of comfort and pride in ignorance.

In our halls, he went on, there were, undeniably, stinks that he knew in his youth, in Cracow, Lodz, and Warsaw. And, on the ground floor, in the dismal rear under the stairwell, if one stood just inside the courtyard door on a windy day, the wind rolling southward would stink of Lithuania.

I told him that I knew nothing about his Lithuanian stink. But he kept on about his stinks, as though they were part of a natural science. It was a ruse to keep me in his kitchen, to accompany his shivering with my own, so that he would not feel quite so miserable. He discussed our street and its contribution toward our atmosphere, which had always given Mildred Osot such grief. To begin with, we had our dead cats, their special value being this: in our neighborhood they can repose for weeks without fear of being molested, or moved. We defer to time, which is our grand decayer, and Tenth Street is unmatched in this observance by any other street in the city. When a cat is about to die it releases its soul to us in the form of its fluids, which trickle toward the curb in a tiny pool, and which often extract from their own elements the beautiful, though oily, colors of a rainbow. Thus, we can hold the cat in memory with a calm assurance of it having been ours, not having stolen into our street from somewhere else just to die. For the soul of a strange cat is bereft of fluid colors entirely. We also had our mutinous children, who frequently soaked a week-old carcass with gasoline, and set it afire, like a smoking pot. We had, too, our historical constituents, which can be said to contribute to the harmony of stinks by their familiarity to us, as if they existed in nature itself, without which we would be lost: the uncollected refuse into which our living cats patiently burrowed, being sinful of long association with impurity; the goods abandoned because of general deterioration, mattresses, bedsprings, clothes, utensils, linoleums, buckets, pots, and boxes, around which congregate the stiffest fumes. We also had the organic deposits of our wine-poisoned tramps, who came nightly into our street in search of crawlspaces, cellar-wells, doorways, and sidewalk grates, long familiar to us as the sources for our richest fermentations. We also had our sewers, our lofts, our very rooms, stinking with human warmth, actual and current in the summer, promissory in the winter.

Thus the hours passed, and our conversation dwindled from monologues to sentences to fragments of thoughts to intermittent words, to silence: it was not yet midnight.

I was engrossed in a book. Bibber, in his chair under the naked light, had been rolling for over an hour his dice-rattle snores. That snore was an adornment of life. I laughed occasionally, out of pure sentiment.

He did not hear my laughter, but he woke immediately from a pounding at the door adjacent to his own.

We went into the hall. Quastafesti was at Tartock's threshold, pleading with the trackwalker for his special sight, his lantern!

"I need your eyes, Tartock! I need your sharp eyes!"

It was Tartock's night off, but he responded without hesitation. He dashed into his rooms for his lantern, his probing stick.

Vincent turned to us. "Barney! Bibber! Help me!"

That tranquil face had collapsed, and those sad eyes were fully expectant of the salt of imminent tears. He brought a rag up to his fleshy nose . . . on the floor beneath us those neighbors whom he'd already alarmed were deep in controversy concerning the wisest course to follow. Vincent's emotion assured a good turnout, despite the hour and the bitter cold.

He was seized by such curious, dry gasps that Bibber clapped at his ears, as if, momentarily, he would lose them to frostbite.

Tartock, lantern and stick in hand, running down the stairs behind us, said: "Of course! Who can afford doctors? We'll find it. We'll find it!"

"It's quite simple," Vincent said to us when we reached the street. "Gilda heard tonight of Osot's dying. You know how she is—you never know what she'll do. Death is a peculiar thing to her—sometimes it sends her off in a bad way. We have a fishknife upstairs, a scaler.

The old man has had it for years. Gilda grabbed hold of it when she got the news about Osot. She just went off, waving this knife. I had to wrestle with her to get it away. She sliced her finger, down to the bone, I think, between the knuckle and the nail. I wrapped up the finger in some toilet paper and rushed her to Bazer, who was just closing. Bazer wound some gauze all round it and sent us off to Bellevue emergency At the clinic the doctor asked for the piece of toilet paper I used before Bazer's gauze. I took him for a madman. He convinced me that he needs the patch of skin for grafting. He says it must be stuck to the toilet paper. We've got to find that patch of skin. I know what he means. Any other kind of surgery will cost too much money. We've got to find that patch of skin."

"I guarantee it!" Tartock said.

"They can't fool me. I know what they mean. It's a matter of money. I know what their gibberish stands for—how much can you pay? Classic exfoliation . . . sensitive papillae . . . depressed cicatrix . . . slough separation . . . no presence of septic material . . . fortunate, fortunate. Yes, the cavity asceptically evacuated . . . ninety-six dollars, please. It's always the same. Poor Gilda. Cellular and tenser tissues, yes, yes . . . obtain apposition of the deeper parts, very good. Bazer doesn't remember the toilet paper. It must be lying somewhere between my shop and his drugstore."

The search proceeded in a harsh, strong wind. Even Arab, Puente's Dalmatian, was out, wheeling and sniffing round thirty pairs of legs. Bibber proclaimed Arab's value to us: the bit of paper would be blood-soaked by now, and could be tracked by scent alone. No plan was formulated. We divided arbitrarily into small groups and followed our eyes. Tartock, with his lantern and his probing stick, led his group into the more difficult alleys and cellar-wells. It was decided that the strong wind had blown the bit of paper into one of a hundred street traps. Tartock passed his lantern over casement and rut and jagged mortice. We were all, in fact, quite thorough. We were aroused, and there was no conceivable thwart to our goal. Quastafesti ran from group to group, holding out to us the mortal hopes of all our street. The possibility of Gilda's quick salvation in the depths of our common indigence gripped him, as it did all of us; it became the single luminary lighting our way, subordinating even Tartock's lantern. A hundred estimates on the cost of special surgery were disallowed. Gilda's own patch of skin would secure the Quastafesti future!

One by one our windows flew open, heads popped out. Our several stores lit up, here at midnight, to offer their portion of light. All those faces discolored by the cold! All those eyes watering, cheeks and noses bitten by the wind! All those arms whipping through the air for warmth.

Tenth Street was being scoured by concomitant hearts. Several homeless hags, beshawled and panting in patchwork rags, squirmed out of mysterious holes to join us. As the minutes passed and nothing turned up a gradual need to calm one another rose up, as if some penalty awaited us if we failed Quastafesti in this search!

Everything portable was overturned—trashcans, boxes and sacks stuffed with junk. Inch by inch our street was sifted through. Stray dogs were attracted to the scene, and they followed Arab. Bibber hurried from place to place, fat and fresh with excitement. He was chilled to the marrow, but he rejoiced. He looked ready to sing! Into every ear sailed his swift opinions on the necessity

for free medicine in America. He was no longer the ves-
tigial curiosity, suspended at a dusty remove from the
center of our human panics. He was participating. He
had thrown off the contemplative life!

To Cahoon, of course, our collaboration was despica-
ble. He lived in ignorance of spontaneous acts; he threw
his discouragements at us as you would feed a flock of
pigeons. He suggested to Bibber that a few pennies
from each of us would defray the cost of surgery, freeing
us of this midnight lunacy. At the door of Quastafesti's
shop the two men fell into a bitter argument; their in-
sults clashed in the icy air. I left them there, two souls
in mutual loathing, each believing he had some special
and secret knowledge of the other, each gnawing with
relish at the other's heart.

I found Vincent in his shop. I closed the door to shut
out the noise of the searchers, which soon diminished to
a vespine buzz. Vincent waded through his swamp of
fabrics, his hair covered with sawdust filler. He thought
it possible that the precious bit of tissue might be here,
in the predictable disorder of his livelihood, since he had
stopped for a sweater on his way to Bazer. He seemed
like himself again with his butcher's block nearby, his
saucy shreds and shirtings, his multiform cartons, his
colored pouches, his golden twine. We turned everything upsidedown. He worried aloud about Gilda and
his father in that dingy clinic at Bellevue, waiting for
word of our success. He explained that he had much to
be thankful for—Gilda's wound might have been worse.
But I was to understand that he had no money, and this
was a force powerful enough to dismantle Tenth Street
for that precious patch of skin. He was not surprised at
our quick reaction to his call. There was never a ques-

tion about an outright refusal on the part of our neighbors! We were too poor to act otherwise! Hence, nothing in our act was shameless.

Here, at the height of his crisis, he spouted formulae! It seemed so foolish! His voice came up from under bags and cartons, old lumber and empty jars, from behind hollow partitions and tinkling pipeage, and his chronicle of neighborhood heroics under the press of money was so calmly developed that he might have been burrowing for merely an old coffee pot or a tarnished spoon.

I turned toward the door. Vincent mistook this for a desire to leave.

"Yago! You think I'm rotten! Well, am I wrong? You think I'm out of my mind! You think that Gilda is my queen materialized under a filthy tiara. You do, don't you? You think I'm not aware how you think of us since Tuesday night? My own sister my mistress, eh? You damned fool! You can't see my performance as just another fishstand? Tell me, do you know of another soul who has put his life in the service of another mortal being? You can't see what it means to restore some sweetness, some balance to a harmless family by casting yourself in a role, though it implies the most terrible thing? Just what are the instruments of your literary art? Your verbatim sight? Kindness? Honesty? Simplicity? Refinement of language? Religion? The Gospels? According to whom? Luke? And all that heard him were astonished at his understanding! John? Ye also ought to wash one another's feet! Maybe the soap we use doesn't suit you, Signor Scrittore! Just what is your pretension? Just what particular dialects are you interested in? And what would you have me do about my irresistible lunatic howling with madness in that dump of a clinic for me to come to her, bearing her miserable patch of skin?"

I could not answer him and he waved a limp hand at my inability to pass a judgment on the spot.

Tartock's smoky lantern was the first thing to appear as Vincent's door flew open. Then Tartock appeared, followed by a pack of neighbors. The flat wick in his lantern was turned up high, throwing off a bright orange-blue light, which took hold and multiplied us threefold in a giant pattern on the walls. Through the open door the icy wind blew at the lantern's flame and whipped our giant shadows into a pathetic dance, Tartock, leading the pack, held his hand out to Vincent.

"Let me be the first to tell you that I was happy to do your dirty work!" he said.

Bibber, Martinez, Bailey, and others stood closely behind Tartock. They were red and puffing and happy. For in Tartock's hand was a soggy, bloody mash of paper. They could hardly restrain themselves before Quastafesti, who gazed mutely at the precious prize. Bibber took out of his pocket a clean white hankerchief, into which Tartock laid the bloody ball.

"You wouldn't believe it," Bibber said. "That rusty little door on the bottom of Kipler's barber pole was open, and somebody kicked it inside the pole, and there Mr. Tartock stuck his lantern, and there he found it!"

"Glad to be of service!" Tartock said.

"And now that you're rich on the money we saved you," Bibber said, "you'll forget your old friends."

"Nothing changes," Vincent said. It was bitterly cold in the doorway draft. Vincent struggled to place a final word into our ears.

"Nothing changes," he said. Then he turned to me

and whispered, "Do you think if we were such a predatory family we'd have such good luck?"

And he ran out of his shop.

SUNDAY

ᗧ ON SUNDAY MORNING, GILDA STATIONED HERSELF AT the front door of our building. All who passed in and out she vexed with her injured finger, now, in its bandage, as big as a squash. Here and there a small dot of blood had appeared. To anyone from whom she failed to solicit attention, she would sing an unintelligible song, and laugh shyly.

I remained in the inner hall for an hour, watching her. At noon, when no one entered or left, she cowered behind the door out of the wind, cradling her bandaged finger in her opposite hand, gazing at it with a twisted face. Her finger had become the new epicenter round which her thoughts could spin. She slowly changed her attitude toward it, and her face untwisted. Soon it assumed a peculiar smile.

She kissed her finger once. She put it into her dirty hair. She swabbed it gently along her arm. She swabbed it along her cheek, as though to elicit from her scratchy skin sympathy for her finger. Presently, she talked to the finger, working her mouth like a broken doll. She put it up to her ear to receive its answers. She nodded her head, and moved her mouth again, assuring the finger she was not immune to its pitiful condition, nor

its hunger—for she then brought it calmly up to her
bosom, in a natural though transitory gesture, and, over
a place on her breast she considered utilizable, she
smoothed her ragged clay-colored coat; in a fit of hy-
genics she spat on her palm and washed with it the
fictive teat. And she put her injured finger there to
suckle.

She saw me. She tried to detain me. But I refused to
acknowledge her. I climbed up to my rooms. I had to
let it go by, as if I had not witnessed her latest rapture.

In fifteen minutes I opened my door to Victor Puente's
knock. Arab was at his legs. Puente's face was contorted,
yet his eyes seemed vacant of expression. He struggled
in his poor English to inform me that his new baby was
dead of ratbites. Difficulties and shyness with our
language had prevented them from seeking immediate
help—they had hoped against hope that the bites were
less serious than was hinted at by the pulpy matter that
had begun on Monday night to gather over the baby's
eye.

Now, Puente's wife would not give up the tiny corpse
to God unless her neighbors moved out of their rooms in
a penance of eviction!

Why? He did not know! Her misery must have de-
ranged her! Puente's voice was toneless, yet under control. He asked me to understand her peculiarity. She
was a simple woman who loved her church. If each tenant carred a few personal belongings out to the curb on
her behalf, she would finally surrender her dead baby; at
least she would be sufficiently diverted so that he might
snatch it away from her.

I fled.

· · ·

It was already dusk when I returned to the corner of Tenth and Avenue C. And when I turned into my street I was sure that my throbbing root had caused me to lose my senses! Dusk and shadow had dragged our buildings to the curbs, twisting them into low, jagged cliffs, running eastward to the river!

It was true! Jagged cliffs of eviction, aswarm with climbers, had shot up, were shooting up before my eyes! Our buildings were turned inside out—they'd all acquiesced to Puente's fantastic plea! Why? I was forced into the gutter, now thronged by luggers and haulers puffing mulishly under tenement packs, . . . and it was a street of near silence! I was shaken more by the indifferent movement than anything else. There was, however, a persistent, elemental sound, a muted hubbub of voices. Most of the cliffbuilders spoke in Spanish, I could not understand them, but I took it all to be the advice they gave one another for the best disposition of their goods. The unique odor of these cliffs boiled into my head like a yellow vapor; it was as if I had wandered into a place I'd never been: a strange, curbside metropole overlooking a yellow bay. I did not realize the extent of this turning out of goods until I reached Quastafesti's shop. There I saw that the cliffs ran to the Jacob Riis circle. Every room on our street must have been emptied out!

"Mr. Artiste! Are you down already?"

It was Bibber, arms laden with clothes, and personal junk, followed by several children, who, in their touching apprenticeship, wished to appear as burdened as he, and bent comically under the few articles he had allowed them to carry.

"You'll excuse me, Mr. Yago, I forgot that you it will

take some time. Well, maybe somebody remembered
your leg and went in and moved you out."

"Have you all gone crazy?"

He ignored me. His movements were apathetic; his
face, a sparkless pan. He directed the children to a particular pile of stuff, instructed them in the proper place-
ment of his religious articles, and sent them back to his
rooms. Then he turned away from me and followed
them into our building. One by one others came out
who were also too preoccupied to exchange a word with
me. The Baileys . . . the Tartocks . . . even Mildred
Osot, who named each thing aloud before she added it
to her place in the line of cliffs.

The swift formation of these cliffs seemed to have no
correspondence with the cliffbuilders, who muled about
without gossip or rant, and who kept piling layer on
layer of stuff onto the curbs with an impassivity, a docil-
ity I'd never seen in them. I could not pull a word out
of anyone! They merely shrugged. I walked up and
down the street and the jagged cliffs kept growing.
They were hard at work, yet their placidity seemed like
a monomania. Cahoon and Judge Merchant were there,
meekly exhibiting leases under the noses of their tenants.
At last His Honor was forced to show himself! The
police had already arrived; they did nothing, for there
was no disturbance. Everyone was calm, perfectly re-
solved. They carried their goods out and constructed
their jagged cliffs as if it was all compatible to their daily
lives, as if they were engaged in a common action that
was good for our street. They were forcing me to admit
that what they were doing was the only possible way, or
else we should all be annihilated!

My mind could not take it all in. The routing out remained free of urgency, and the goods kept coming. They worked with such competence that they moved about as though on padded slippers. They had stopped advising each other, so that now even their muted babble was gone. I saw Bibber accompany his cousin, Baron (who had been visiting him all day), along the opposite curb. Baron was fully involved with the prominence given to a series of refrigerator doors, which were removed from their hinges in accordance with a certain statute of safety in our city code, and which were set upright against the lines of cliffs, giving them a vertical, mansard appearance. To Baron it seemed that the sole object of these events was to provide him with desirable items.

At last I saw Puente's wife. She came out of our building and walked to her particular pile of stuff. She climbed over protruding crags of furniture and sat herself high atop the cliff, on an inverted bucket, resting her feet on a whiteboard box. Her new baby was cradled in her bosom. She wept quietly. Puente was unable to comfort her. He perched before her on his knees upon a rolled mattress pressed down by his own weight, together with that of a shattered trunk. He gazed upward at his wife, at her tiny bundle, and neither of them would budge, as though they were lashed to the multitude of things beneath them.

Arab's grief had taken the form of a tight wheeling round his master's pile of goods. He squealed pathetically, as if the wheel of his madness squealed. The presence of that tiny bundle at the bosom of his mistress could not drive the poor dog on too swiftly, he kept going and going, it seemed that at any moment he would, by centrifugal thrust, achieve a radical separation of his

markings from his silky white coat, to ultimately iso-
late Puente's goods in a whirling torque of black spots.

Soon a crowd gathered, drawn to the spectacle of a
dog ringing his master in. Many were not from our
street; I'd seen a crowd of people drawn to the scene
from the buildings west of Avenue C, and some had
come from Avenue A, picking up new people as they
passed through Avenue B, with that expanding ferment
of people moving toward immediate participation in
some unknown tragedy. But many of the spectators
were people of our own street, worn out, resigned to
their new curbside residence.

Cahoon nudged me from behind. He handed me my
rent receipt. Finally, finally. Quastafesti, who had emptied out his shop, edged toward me and poured his
broken thoughts into my ear: "Look how the bones are
exposed! We're out of our wallets, yes, *sir*. Look at poor
Arab, his heart'll burst. Fatten us in our coops of mud,
then send in your rats. That'll diminish our numbers.
What's to be done? One has to cooperate. Spare us this
Christian infant, oh, Jesus, with half of its face in a rat's
belly."

Esther Cahoon, holding little Jenny's hand, nervously
moved into the circle, and I heard her say to Quastafesti:
"Imagine holding on to that infant since Monday morning not being able to make heads nor tails out of English, and what do they expect, not making an effort,
and what do we expect, not caring an ounce?"

And then, unexpectedly, Puente's wife rose. She sur-
veyed our street. She studied this crowd of her neighbors. She studied Arab's whirl round her pile of goods.
She studied her husband. She studied this estrepement
of tenants who had so prejudiced themselves in the eyes

of the law. Checked, in the end, by her own numbness of mind, longing for the conclusion of her dog's mad whirling, she made her way down off her jagged cliff and passed among the circle of spectators. Puente took the baby from her, so that she herself became a spectator. He clutched it to his own breast now. He rocked back and forth, back and forth, as if there was some indefinite force in him which even he did not understand. Tears spilled from his eyes, but he made no sound. Arab leaped up but failed to snag the tiny bundle. The dog then sprawled, exhausted, at the legs of his mistress, his head keeled over his forelegs, his steaming tongue flapping at the cold pavement. Puente undid the top folds of the white-hemmed blanket, and exposed the beautiful baby's face. Puente handed the tiny corpse to Bibber, who looked at it, and handed it to Baron. Baron, in turn, handed it to Esther Cahoon. Little Jenny stood on her toes to gaze at the baby's face. Mildred Osot took it next, then handed it to Bailey. I hurried away. I went into our building and its bastard light. Every door was open. Our entire building was out on the street, every room was empty, disgorged, every stick and nibble of my neighbors had been stacked upon the curbs!

But my own rooms at least were filled. I was in possession of the final repository of warmth, of stability and order in a decaying tower of bare cells.

But no! My door was open along with all the others, and my rooms as empty! Who could have taken it on themselves to invade my rooms and banish my stuff with theirs quite naturally and as a matter of course?

On the way down I determined to retrieve my things by dismantling, piecemeal, if necessary, the entire line of jagged cliffs, starting from D and working westward to C.

When I reached the street I saw that they were standing round Puente's pile of goods just as I had left them!
The tiny corpse was still being aired! While the police
tried to ascertain from Puente the details of his child's
death, our neighbors could not surrender the tiny bundle to the green mortuary van waiting at the corner.
Some spark of their own lives was contained in the
corpse of this child. They bore the same relation to it
now as its mother had borne before. Puente, in his
stumbling tongue, provided them with the inner force
to pass his child from hand to hand, as if the motion
itself would bring a miracle. The gray gelatinous bubble
of matter in the socket of the baby's right eye had begun to emit the stench of decomposition; the baby's face
was swollen, its hair a wet pad, a weak shine was on its
skin . . . yet not a soul had turned away.

I was handed the baby, and I looked at it. I gave it to
Judge Merchant.

"I am not a beast, Mr. Yago," he said.

"No, your Honor, . . . the rat who feasted on this
baby's face is the beast!"

Neither my absence nor my return had been noticed.
I was simply there. And so, because a power had risen
in this tiny corpse to demand satisfaction, it rode the
ring of our arms round and round . . . for I don't
know how many turns.

A NOTE ABOUT THE AUTHOR

EDWARD ADLER, whose many jobs reflect a traditional pattern among American writers, has been at various times a counter-man, a chauffeur, a technical book editor and a fur worker; he has put in stints, too, as a technical writer, grocer, draftsman and cab driver. A first lieutenant in the Air Force during World War II, he served for three years in Europe with the Troop Carrier Command. Born in 1920 in New York City, he is married to the former Elaine Lipton and is the father of a three-year-old son. Mr. Adler is presently at work on his second novel.

A NOTE ON THE TYPE

THE TEXT of this book is set in GRANJON, a type named in compliment to Robert Granjon, type-cutter and printer—Antwerp, Lyons, Rome, Paris—active from 1523 to 1590. The boldest and most original designer of his time, he was one of the first to practice the trade of type-founder apart from that of printer. This type face was designed by George W. Jones, who based his drawings on a type used by Claude Garamond (1510-61) in his beautiful French books, and more closely resembles Garamond's own than do any of the various modern types that bear his name.

Composed, printed, and bound by H. Wolff, New York.
Paper manufactured by P. H. Glatfelter Co.,
Spring Grove, Pennsylvania.
Typography by Vincent Torre

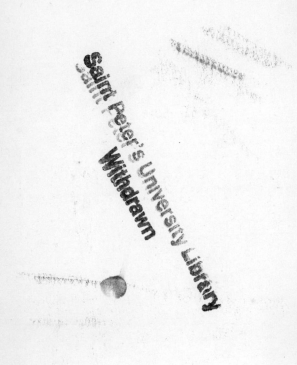